BIRYANIYAT

Tales from the city of Biryani...

Anthology Vol. 2

BIRYANIYAT

Curators

Sirisha Naidu
Aruna Kumar

Editor

Lavanya Nukavarapu

EKA PUBLISHERS
#118 Ushodaya Enclave, PO Miyapur
Hyderabad 500049 (India)
ekapresshyderabad@gmail.com
+91 8008101590
www.ekapress.org

A Paperback original 2021

Compilation by Eka Publishers 2021

Copyright © owned by Eka Publishers and HydRAW

ISBN: 978-81-944712-5-7
FICTION

Cover Image: Farheen Moulana
Set in Sabon by Eka Publishers
Printed and bound in India by Eka Publishers

PUBLISHER'S NOTE

We are proud to present, BIRYANIYAT, our second anthology in association with HydRAW team after the grand success of the first book, ADVENT, launched last year. BIRYANIYAT is yet another effort by the team of HydRAW and EKA to bring the best stories from the city of Biryani, Hyderabad. This time we have contributing authors from different parts of the country.

Anthologies are a favourite of readers. For starters, they are quick reads. One can read the book at a stretch or by taking breaks between stories. An anthology is a great gifting option to your book lover friend as you don't have to worry if your friend will like the story or not. Since there are plenty of stories, your friend will never be disappointed.

EKA Publishers was setup by a group of experts with clear vision of supporting upcoming authors and make publishing easy and affordable for all. We firmly believe that a book is a result of lot of hard work and so publishing should be easy. EKA's USP is to provide customized options to our authors which is unmatched by any other publisher.

HydRAW is a sanctuary for all interested in reading and writing, formed with the objective to be a bridge between readers and writers. The book is at the centre of its mission.

With Biryaniyat we are one more step closer to our mission to bring the best from the upcoming authors and future bestselling authors of India. We hope you like reading this as much as we did putting it together.

Smriti Karn
Publishing Director, EKA Publishers

FOREWORD

Short stories are a great reflection of the human society. Incidents occurring in our daily lives take an interesting turn when authors describe them in the form of a short story. The way we live, our behaviour, happy moments and fears; all emotions have been well depicted in this anthology 'Biryaniyat.'

Travelling through this anthology, readers get to explore many facets of life and experience different cultures. As they say, shades of life - it is very well described in the bouquet of short stories present in this anthology.

In the second anthology of HydRAW, each and every story has a unique touch and will be a pleasant reading experience for the readers. A few contributors have tasted successes as their stories have featured in HydRAW's first anthology 'Advent' as well.

I am sure readers will be immersed in varied experiences with each story. Different emotions beautifully expressed by the characters may turn nostalgic and take you down the memory lane.

Through Advent, HydRAW kick started the publishing journey for budding and previously published authors. Biryaniyat furthers the journey of HydRAW of giving a platform to writers from all across India to reach a wider audience.

I wish that all the contributing authors grow exponentially as writers. May they have a glorious writing career!

- Devika Das

Devika Das is an award-winning author, poet and actor from the city of Hyderabad. Her recent title 'The Mind Game' has been promoted from Self-Publishing to Traditional Publishing. Now, the title is published by Hesten Publishers. She is a professional Content Writer wherein she writes on topics related to IT and Emerging Technologies. To know more about Devika's writing ventures, please visit www.authordevika.com

Contents

SENGANTHAL MALAR

Gautam Sasidharan

As the white Omni sped ahead on the road, one could see the vast areas of vacant lands on both sides, dotted with nothing but palm trees. Occasionally, one would spot some greenery announcing the arrival of a village. Occasionally, a tea shop would be spotted on the banks of the road, decorated with cracked wooden benches, strips of paper, plastic covers and *beedi* stubs. Yet tea would be the last thing one would want to drink, as the sun beat down and evaporated every drop of water.

Oddanchatram. That was the name of the place where we were heading to. We were visiting a friend's place, a sought after excuse to while away time during our college days. My reverie was broken by my friend's booming voice, asking for directions. After a few turns, the car was parked alongside the road. Inferring it as a cue for attending nature's call, I jumped out of the car, only to be surprised by our friend, Pandi, waiting for us.

My friend from Oddanchatram was a temple statue personified; black in colour, sturdy in build. But his most admirable feature was not the gentle smile but a beaming one, displaying a pearl white band against a black backdrop. Sometimes, this display had a greater pleasing effect than a cute smile of a child. Such was his aura. To top it, there was a mass of black hair, speckled with strands of white.

As we followed him along the trodden pathways of what seemed to be dry arid land, he explained the features of the place. We could see that the land wasn't unused. The vast land was divided into many plots; most were ploughed while some were flecked with ash. It was that time of the year when one had to wait for the rains or for the irrigation canals to fill. Once this criterion was met the ploughed fields would be sown and the area would once again become lush green suppressing the beauty of the long and winding roads.

As we approached the middle of this expanse of land, we were ushered into a house which was neither out of place, like a big mansion, nor in place, like a hut. Outside, we were greeted at the courtyard by Pandi's beaming old grandmother. We all took seats around her on the stringed cot and asked her wellbeing. In an effort to bring down the sun's torture, a mud pot of buttermilk was passed around by Pandi's mother. As the tangy taste hit the taste buds and traversed the food pipe before hitting the abyss of our stomachs, a sensation beyond words arose inside the skull.

After a moderate lunch and an afternoon siesta, we started roaming the area around the house. From a distance, we could hear the sound of children shouting in glee. As we went closer, we could see boys waiting and jumping into a wide pit. It revealed itself to be a water body, which served as an underground well as well as a natural pool. The boys were taking turns to jump, exhibiting their somersaulting skills. My mind would have set about on a verbose pejorative of the apathy towards the tremendous skills of rural India had it not been for this curious plot of land which lay beyond.

It was not the land that attracted me, but the occupants. I walked towards the land without anybody's company. But, Pandi was silently following me, leaving the others to bask in the waters in the company of the boys. The plot was fenced with barbed wires and the occupants were plants, neatly planted in rows, as in a plantation. The highlight of these plants was the flower, Senganthal Malar. Until then, I had not heard of such a flower. Those were the days of Nokia 1100 and hence I had to rely on Pandi's knowledge.

Gloriosa Superba or Senganthal Malar, is the state flower of Tamil Nadu. Its complexion is unique, setting about with a yellow in the base and slowly working towards a red at the fringes; giving vivid imagery of a flame. Every part of this plant is poisonous; and as is with every poison, a measured amount is used for medicinal purposes. This unique feature gives the plant a high commercial value, and is hence cultivated.

As I stood admiring the beautiful flowers, Pandi walked towards the farthest corner of the land. Amongst the plants, arose a boy of our age who could have easily passed for a girl, with a striking similarity to Pandi. I had no idea that my friend had a twin. They both walked towards me. I extended my arm as an introduction and was surprised when he introduced himself as Kanthal in his language, Sinhalese Tamil.

Pandi saw my bewildered expression and ushered me to sit on the bund. The sun was on its downward journey and a gentle breeze blew down the Ghats bringing along the smell of brewed chicory coffee.

Years before, when Pandi was a toddler, he used to have a ravenous appetite; not that it has subsided now. On that particular night, Pandi was woken up by a grumble in his stomach. Finding nothing in the house to lay his hands upon, he moved outside. It was a moonlit night, a wilder night, filled with snakes, mongooses, porcupines and the likes on the prey. Earlier that day, he had seen somebody digging the soil beneath the plant with the red flower and take away the tuber.

Encouraged by this memory, Pandi moved towards the plant and was delighted to find the remaining tubers freshly dug. He picked one of them and was going to dig in, when a hand hit hard against it, sending the tuber flying. He was caught unaware by the sudden attack and a fury of emotions rising from the gut, moving towards the brain, as was evident from the movement of his Adam's apple. Before he could say anything, a sweet girlish voice spoke in the darkness, warning him that it was poisonous.

The sudden commotion had everybody up in the house, and they caught the intruder, a boy who spoke in some different dialect. On a rather fruitless enquiry, it was inferred that he was a refugee who had lost his way from family and life. Ever since, he had become a member of Pandi's family. It was he who introduced Pandi's family to the business of this flowering plant and ensuing commercial prosperity.

That day, as I fell asleep staring at the ceiling of Pandi's house I had no idea of the remaining part of the story.

Coincidentally, years after that wonderful trip I met my friend Pandi again, unfortunately, among the cold benches of a hospital; both of us attending to our wives' pregnancies. We had not made it to each other's marriages and hence went to meet our respective families. As the face of his wife came into view, I was overcome by a feeling of similarity. I couldn't speak anything, for the person in front of me was Kanthal but in female attire. Once again it was my friend's turn to explain the situation.

When the intruder was caught on that night, everyone in the neighbourhood had assumed that it was a boy. As the commotion died, Pandi's family came to know that it was a girl. In order to save her from society and to suppress any further questions, Pandi had efficiently disguised her as a boy. When it became difficult to hide her identity, they sent her out of the town and later brought her back into the family in her true identity and as Pandi's wife.

As Pandi completed his narration, I had nothing to say. It was difficult to accept all that he had said, but then, I went by Pandi's words. I faced Pandi's wife and asked her, "Vanakkam, what is your name?"

"Senganthal Malar".

Intrigued by the name, I googled, only to discover that Kanthal and Senganthal Malar identify the same plant, the same flower.

THE TRAIL

Krishna Ahir

The boy walked through the forest, admiring the glistening of the snow on the branches of the trees. He was checking the traps his father had laid out the day before last, hoping they'd be able to have seconds for dinner. This winter has been harsh, and with three children sick in bed, it was up to the father and his youngest son to procure more supplies. So far none of the traps had caught anything. He coughed as he continued down the trail.

Finding the last of the traps triggered but empty, the boy was about to turn and head home when a splash of colour caught his eye. He crouched and inspected the drop of red, stark against the white of the snow. Blood, still fresh, led away from the trap into the forest. The boy hesitated. If he left now, he would reach home just before the sun set and the temperature plummeted. If he followed the trail, there was a possible meal waiting. Thinking a nice warm meal would help his siblings recover faster, he stood to follow the trail, and the world spun, and he fell to his knees. He'd stood up too fast, in his excitement. When he regained his balance, he stood up again and moved forward.

The further he followed the blood, the colder the air became. The sun was setting, and the boy realized that he was the farthest from home he had ever been. There was no chance of coming home before dark. His father would be both worried and angry that the boy had taken so long. He hoped the blood belonged to a large animal, so that the promise of a few good meals would appease him. The trees thinned until he reached a wide field, with a blanket of snow undisturbed but for the scarlet drops of blood that led to a large tree. His heart skipped a beat.

The boy had never seen a stranger tree. The bark shimmered gold, and the lower branches spiralled around the trunk, with leaves that were blue at the stem, fading into purple and then red, which fell onto the snow with a steady drip, drip, drip. The higher branches were twisted, curving up to form a large sphere. With a start, the boy realized that the blood he had been following wasn't blood at all - it seemed to be some sort of sap, coming from the tree, but how was it possible? The tree couldn't have moved with its roots buried in the ground, and the boy realized that while following the blood-like sap there had been no other prints in the snow beside his own.

Drawing closer to the tree, he reached up and brushed his hand against one of the leaves, pulling it away to inspect the sap now covering his fingers. It smelled sweet, and tasted of a fruit that the boy could not name but felt distantly familiar. Gathering more of the sap to taste again, he tried to recall just where he had encountered this flavour before. The more he drank, the more familiar it became. It was on the tip of his tongue, both literally and figuratively. Glaring up at the tree as he tried to figure it out, the boy saw that the sphere of branches had relaxed, now forming a loose weave with small gaps. Through the gaps he caught sight of a woman sitting in the cradle the branches formed.

The boy called out to her, but she didn't respond. She was swaying back and forth as if listening to a silent song only she could hear. He grabbed one of the lowest branches and hoisted himself up to straddle it. The woman had noticed him now, peering down at him with delighted eyes. She looked very beautiful, he thought. She also looked very lonely, and the boy decided he ought to keep her company for a little while, before he went back home. She smiled at him and ran a finger down one of the branches she sat upon, and one of the gaps grew larger and larger until it formed a doorway into the wooden net that made up the sphere of the tree.

He continued climbing the tree, the branches growing closer and closer together until they were a staircase leading to the top of the tree. A low humming reached his ears, and he recognized it as the lullaby his mother would sing to him when he was sick as a very small child, before she passed away of illness herself. When he reached the doorway, the woman was waiting for him. The boy wondered how long she'd been there alone, and why she didn't look cold even with no cloak on, in the middle of winter. She waved a hand, gesturing for him to come inside. He suddenly realized he had forgotten all about his original goal of finding a meal for him and his family. His stomach growled, and the woman took a step back to reveal the inside of the sphere, where a pot of what looked like a meaty stew sat, giving off a light steam. He licked his lips. After the meal he would ask if he could take the leftovers with him when he went home, he decided. The woman smiled larger, and reached out a hand in invitation. The boy smiled back at her and accepted it.

The father held his youngest son's wrist loosely in his grasp, desperately searching for a beat. When he'd found his youngest son collapsed of fever by the last of the traps, he'd gathered the boy in his arms and rushed back home to lay him down next to his brothers. All three of them had come down with the same sickness. It had looked as if it had passed the youngest by, but then he had been hit the hardest. His fever had spiked drastically, hot enough that the father believed that his hand would burn when he checked the boy's forehead. When his heart had stopped beating, the father had frantically performed chest compressions for what seemed like hours, praying with all his heart that his son to survive.

He couldn't find a pulse. His son's wrist lay cold and limp in his hands. The father started weeping, bent over his son's body. It didn't look like a corpse at all. With his eyes closed and face still, he looked as if he was merely sleeping, like his brothers. The father dreaded the morning, when he would have to tell his sons that their brother was dead. He sat there crying for what seemed like an eternity. After a long pause, he stood up, making no move to wipe the tears still falling off his face.

Scooping the body in his arms, he moved his son over to the table, and rummaged around the house until he found a clean sheet to cover him with. Glancing back as he moved towards the door, the father hoped his son was met with a warm welcome by the mother he had barely known. He grabbed his shovel. Although he would wait until his sons have said their goodbyes, it would be best to start the preparations now. He opened the door to be greeted by the coming dawn. Still weeping, the father stepped outside to dig his youngest son's grave.

SHOULDERS

Muralidharan Parthasarathy

December 20th, 2015, 2 AM IST.

"*Yeh aapne kya kar diya Sardarji*[1]?" Arun almost yelled and the giant truck came to a screeching halt.

"What happened, Bro? What do you think? Is this your Maruti 800 to stop anywhere at your whim and fancy? Turn and take a look." Before the driver could complete his sentence, the nonstop honking of buses, lorries, and cars from behind resounded. Streams of two wheelers sieved through.

"Arun," continued Sardar changing the gears, "This is not your Trichy City Street. This is NH 47," and the truck moved forward.

"*Dei, erumamadu. Thadiya*[2]," the passing vehicle's drivers furiously scolded the Sardar in Tamil. Only Arun could understand the meaning and not the Sardar. The monster truck had occupied nearly three lanes of the National Highway from Trichy to Chennai leaving little room for any other vehicle to overtake. Vehicles rolled like snails to avoid brushing the giant truck.

"Oh Sardarji! We missed a crucial left turn to *Athur* half a kilometre behind," Arun informed the Sardar in a distressed tone.

---

[1] *Yeh aapne kya kar diya Sardarji?* ---What have you done Sardarji?
[2] *Dei, erumamadu. Thadiya* ---Hey buffalo fatso!

"Aren't you a local? You could have told me before, Arun. Luckily, there is a Truck Bay very nearby." Sardar responded, annoyed and irritated.

Arun sweated in spite of the chilly breeze. He was so tensed that he couldn't sight the truck bay Sardar had mentioned. Sardar slowed down, swerving and manoeuvring the vehicle diligently left into the curve like bay. He then shut the engine, opened the door, and climbed down the small ladder below. He stretched his hands and looked listlessly trying to gauge what had gone wrong.

* * * * *

21 Hours GMT London.

Hi dad!"

Hello James. Did you watch WWE today?"

"Yeah, only for a short while because I had FIFA 2016 games installed on my laptop. I played that."

"That's great."

"Your voice is feeble and is cutting off."

"Yeah, I am in a moving car on an Indian highway on the way to my project site."

"Did you see snake charmers? Monkeys? Elephants?"

"Maybe, but I don't recall now."

"Why, dad? Are you suffering from memory loss?"

"Not at all. Am in a crisis, dude."

"What's a crisis?"

"Sorry, I often forget that you are just a six-year old. Let me try an example. You have just loaded FIFA 16, and if your play station crashes, it can be considered a crisis."

"That's a blow. Like the massive one they show in WWE."

"Yeah. I am right now in one such soup."

"Who gave you the blow? Didn't you call the cops?"

"Not physical but a setback in the business plan."

"You lost? An elephant came in your way?"

"No, I'll send you some visuals so that you get the scenario."

"Visuals of?"

"Of the giant truck."

"Like the one James Bond drives in 'Casino Royale'?"

"Maybe a little bigger. Just wait. You will see later."

"Can't you send them now?"

"I haven't reached there yet."

"Okay."

Neil Morgan was in no mood to talk to the chauffeur. There was no use either. The people in this rural belt of Tamil Nadu couldn't decipher anything he spoke. One of the local men on the site who understood English informed the driver where to go.

Neil opened his laptop and drafted an e-mail.

Charles, this is no good news. One goddamn Indian truck driver omitted a left turn in a major Cross Road in NH 47, messing up the delivery of 1000 m3 boiler from Bharat Heavy Electricals Ltd., Trichy. It must have reached the site anytime now, i.e. clear 24 hours ahead of the trial run by Romano Corp Installation team. Needless to say the Russians are ruthless. Jesus! This is going to cost us dearly. Romano Corp will demand £10K for every extra day. Sadly, the next traffic intersection capable with the width to allow this monster is a solid 30 km away and with restrictions for its movement during the day time. It will start moving after 15 more hours from now. Charles, you assigned me a dream project, but my bad luck is after me.

Nevertheless, please ask the Legal Team to send a notice by email to the hopeless Indian Logistics Firm, making it clear we would sue them for damages. Let them learn to deploy an educated driver in future. I will send a PowerPoint presentation on the next action plan for the 'Trial Run' with photos of the stranded truck.

Regards, Neil.

* * * * *

But for the light in the bedroom, the house was pitch dark.

"Should you go now? Can't you accompany me to the doctor? The dispensary will open only by 10," Kumaran's wife clad in a housecoat pleaded with her husband in a hushed voice lest the child might wake up.

"Look Selvi, our Kavya is already seven years old. She should be able to withstand the fever," Kumaran replied dressing up for duty, "Keep me updated." He closed the door, switched on the torch of his mobile phone, and slowly reached the shoe rack near the front door.

He knelt to take out his pair from a heap of slippers on a small shoe rack, "Velan, leaving so early?" His mother's voice came from the corner of an otherwise dark living room. "It's an emergency, ma. I am rushing to the highway."

"You came so late last night, Velan. If you strain like this, you might fall sick."

Without responding to her, he closed the door, and the 'wroom' of his motorcycle scathed through the quiet chill night of the village.

* * * * *

"Wow, dad! What a giant truck that is!" James exclaimed.

"Fifteen meters long and three meters wide."

"Dad, the trailer has twelve tires in all six more tyres below the truck. There is something on the trailer, which looks like a giant Egyptian Mummy Pot."

"That is called a boiler; it withstands any heat."

"Is your job chasing trucks?"

"No dude. I track trucks to make sure my business goes on time. Do you know how I took the video when there was no light?"

"The giant vehicle is clearly visible."

"I used the rented car's headlights."

"Cool!"

"It's very late. Aren't you going to bed?"

"Very excited about FIFA 16. Trying so many new games."

"Is Mom home? What did you have for dinner?"

"I ate a burger. Mom was late but got busy doing 'On-Call-Duty' in her room."

"No choice, she has to do that once in a month. Why don't you sleep now, James?"

"Okay, it was fun watching the giant Indian Truck."

Fun for him! Neil didn't know what to do now. Somehow he couldn't move ahead. The truck driver and his escort were chitchatting in the cabin. The chauffeur had pushed back his seat and fell asleep. Headlights were still on.

Suddenly, a motorcycle appeared from nowhere. Neil waved away the insects that entered the car when he lowered to see why a motorcycle was coming near the truck. More flies were swarming the beam of light from the headlights of the car. The motorcyclist first blinked due to the excessive glare. After parking his motorcycle away from the truck in a corner, he neared the car and mildly knocked on the window. As Neil lowered the window glass, he wished, "Good morning, Neil Sir. I'm Kumaran."

"Whoever you are, why are you showing up your face after the fate is sealed? Don't you have any sense? What were the goddamn logistic idiots doing? Look young man, you have already derailed my dream. But it's going to cost your corporate a bomb," bellowed Neil.

There was no reaction perceivable in the dim light reflected on Kumaran's face as he bent forward to listen intently.

"Are you mute? Speak up, man," Neil's voice rose in pitch much to his astonishment.

"Unable to understand, sir."

"What the hell you don't understand?"

"You speak too fast."

Neil pounced his head on the rear of the front seat, "To hell with you Indians. You want all FDI but have no business acumen and don't even know simple English."

Kumaran stood in silence.

Neil's frustration mounted. No use talking to this fellow either, he thought. The truck stood hopelessly idle in the car's headlight illumination.

"Do you read English?"

"Yes sir."

"Get inside," Neil moved to his right and opened his laptop. Kumaran got into the car and sat with a sufficient distance from Neil.

Neil pointed at the mail to Charles, "Read this."

Kumaran read it fully and finally replied, "I have informed my office, sir."

What easy disposal! It's impossible to handle this lot. Both of them sat in silence for a few minutes. Neil pondered. He couldn't possibly leave it to this idiot.

"Do one thing. Let's go to the guest house in the site in *Athur*," he talked as slowly as he could lest the guy doesn't blink again.

Kumaran nodded and Neil patted heavily on the driver's shoulder. The driver woke up and looked around. He opened the door, came out, and stretched. Then he knelt forward a bit and peeked inside the car and took out a water bottle, turned around, went forward a few steps, and washed his face.

The insects were now more in number; seeing Neil driving them out with great difficulty, Kumaran raised the window glasses. Then he got out of the car and went up to the truck cabin using the ladder and had a word or two with Sardarji and Arun there. Then he returned to the car and took his seat. In his preoccupation, Neil didn't notice it had dawned, but the fog was not allowing the Sun to show up. Kumaran talked to the driver, and the car moved.

Neil noted the time of their leaving the 'Truck Bay'. It was 7.30 AM IST.

By 7.50, the car took a U-turn in a major traffic intersection just ahead of the next toll plaza. Neil could gauge this would be the point where the truck might take a U-turn to reach the site. As he could see from the back seat, the car was speeding at 80 km per hour which meant in those 20 minutes it must have crossed around 27 km. Just for that, the truck had to wait a whole day.

When would the Indians lay 16 lane highways? 8 lanes can never handle these. Suddenly, the car slowed down after Kumaran told something to the driver in Tamil. The car turned left into the service lane. After ten minutes' drive, it halted somewhere.

"I will go to the temple," without waiting for Neil's reply Kumaran got down. The driver followed him. They entered a small temple with a multi-coloured dome. Out of curiosity Neil got down to have a look and stopped outside the temple near the peacock statue which faced the deity inside.

The deity's face was decorated with sandalwood paste. An adorned spear rested on the statue's right shoulder. Many garlands, pink and white in colour embellished the deity.

A priest held a plate with a small flame on a brass plate in front of the deity and moved it thrice, up and down in clockwise circles. Then he held the plate in front of the two men. Both of them gestured touching the flame with the right palm and devotedly touched their eyes with the palm. They prostrated in front of the sanctum in the narrow space and came out.

Neil was inside the car ahead of them. The carbon in the air was rising. The nonstop honking by drivers of various vehicles and the sound of friction of tyres were deafening. Neil noticed both had put some white powder on their forehead in the temple.

The car sped towards the site, and involuntarily, Neil looked for the truck on the other side of highway, and he sighted it too.

The gloom was getting darker over him. Charles, his boss would be promoted as Vice President. Neil was the best choice for them to position him as GM (Global Projects) so far. But this setback could reverse everything. Would these Indians comprehend how it hurts when you lose something you so well deserve, but someone else spoilt it casually?

After reaching the site Neil retired to his room. The chef in the guest house was an amateur. Bread, omelette with pepper and packed sauce, which Neil had brought from London, was the only manageable breakfast for him. Kumaran waited in the lobby.

After breakfast Neil checked mail. Charles had replied, "It's all in the game, but the finance team's reaction will be a pain in the ass."

A knock on the door woke him up. The chef bowed, "Lunch is ready sir." It was 2 p.m. IST.

Neil felt the heat outside when he looked for Kumaran in the lobby. He was missing. Maybe he had gone for lunch. Why the staff didn't offer him lunch, Neil wondered. He was in no mood to eat anything. He chose cucumber, capsicum, and onion from the salads and ate French fries and fried chicken with grape juice for dessert.

It was 3 p.m. IST and there was no sight of Kumaran. By 4 p.m., Neil became nervous. Leaving a cushion of 12 hours for the slow mover, will the truck reach at least late-night tomorrow?

Where is that guy? He called the site staff. Luckily, one of them who always picked, and spoke English well picked his phone this time as well. Neil asked him to track down Kumaran.

By 4.30 p.m., Neil got the feedback. Kumaran was on the highway, and the truck may move anytime. How could it move in the four-lane congestion? Is he trying to fool me? What is he up to, to entangle me into an accident of this truck on the highway?

Neil put on his formals and headed towards the highway. The intersection was 20 km away. Ironically there was no traffic between the intersection and the site in the four-lane road.

As the car neared the site, he found four young men on the left with a placard that read 'Heavy boiler truck reversing. Emergency. Please slow down'. Many buses cars and vans were waiting to take a left into the highway ahead of his.

Neil alighted. Bracing the unendurable heat and dust, he moved forward.

What is the game plan of this Kumaran? Neil slowly understood. Instead of waiting till midnight and then moving slowly and doing the U-turn which might thwart the crucial deadline of the project, this man is reversing the giant truck in day light itself. Neil wondered how a stream of vehicles, buses, lorries and cars alike were co-operating. How Kumaran managed to rope in a traffic constable?

Traffic was on the move on the other side of the highway only. On this side where the truck was taking the left, to Neil's right, he found a big string of vehicles honking. A traffic policeman was helping the 'placard holding' boys and some others. Without the traffic policeman there was no one regulating the traffic this side.

Suddenly, the constable whistled, and a human chain of ten boys in the middle of the four lanes in which the truck was reversing, allowing only one vehicle at a time. Neil started walking in the service lane to his left on the highway.

He could not believe his eyes. The giant truck was on a reverse mode and hardly fifty feet away from the intersection.

When the truck reversed the entire traffic stopped for ten minutes. The truck kept on moving backward. Then the truck was stopped for ten minutes, and only one vehicle was allowed to overtake the truck.

Kumaran was holding a stick with a red rag tied on top of it near the front side of the truck to its right. When he raised the pole with the flag, the traffic was stopped by the traffic constable at a visible distance.

As Neil watched awestruck, in an hour the truck reached the intersection, and it took another 15 minutes for it to turn sharply left and slowly head towards the site.

Standing near his car, not used to the pollution, Neil coughed heavily. Lifting a bottle from the car he poured water on his face and wiped his perspiration with a tissue paper that turned nearly black. He threw it into the trash.

Kumaran came with the traffic constable, and the latter saluted Neil. "Thanks, officer," Neil shook hands with him. The cop replied in Tamil, which Neil couldn't follow. He shook hands again and got into his car.

Jesus! How fortune turned topsy-turvy in one day. He sent a brief mail, "Charles, issue resolved. The trial run will be on the dot tomorrow. Thumbs up!"

He wanted to call James, but he must have been asleep by then, so he dropped the idea. In guest house after a bath he switched on Star Sports Channel on the Television. "Wow, Manchester United vs Liver Pool." He poured some vodka in a glass and sipped.

By 8.30 PM, the giant had entered the site. Specially made railings were pulled out for the truck to roll on. Workers assembled near a crane that would safely move the boiler into the 100ft — height shop.

Kumaran, with folded hands said, "Good Night, sir."

"Not yet!" Neil who was taller than Kumaran put his right hand on Kumaran's shoulders and escorted him.

"Take your seat Kumaaraan," he pointed to the sofa. Hesitantly Kumaran sat down.

Neil took out champagne, ice cubes and glasses and set them on the dining table. "Come on. Let's celebrate the whole night."

"Sorry, sir, but I need to go home now."

"Come on. You achieved a big thing. Let's celebrate. Home can always wait."

There was no smile on the young man's face.

"My daughter is running a high fever."

Neil talked very slowly, "Is someone with her? Has she seen the doctor?"

Kumaran replied with a grim face, "She won't fall asleep till I reach home. She sleeps only on my shoulders." His face was black with vehicle pollution and sweat, and he looked exhausted.

"Ok," Neil responded hesitantly. "Take my car."

"Thank you, sir. But I have my motorcycle with me."

Neil shook hands with Kumaran and embraced him. He was surprised that the pungent smell of sweat didn't bother him at all. Kumaran left.

Within moments, Neil felt he could have given him at least a hundred pounds as tips. He rushed to the parking lot, but Kumaran's vehicle was wrooming past the main gate.

THE UNHEARD VOICES

Pranay Mathur

Ashish rushed out of his bungalow unable to take in the mass of scarlet that met his eyes as he entered his house. His furniture, gleaming red, basking in the sun's bright rays, his tiles, splattered with blood, and his threshold, covered with the red footprints of his conscience, were too much for him to take. He slammed the door shut, separating his cool rational mind from the voices within, and raced out into his wide garden, dotted with red carnations.

He walked over to the bed, plucking out the eerily blood-red flowers and tearing them to shreds. He sat down on the cool grass, ruining his three-piece suit, as he loosened his tie and buried his face in his palm.

Ashish was a man in his late forties, an illustrious lawyer with a successful business and a renowned name. Lawyers dreaded him, criminals adored him, and onlookers could only watch in awe as he wove out a story and interrogated witnesses, pointing out weaknesses and capturing both the jury as well as the judge with his well-researched arguments. His sharp, square-jawed face, with his dark brown eyes and jet black hair with the neat side-parting, coupled with his crisp suit and tie, seemed to radiate a sense of knowledge and power.

But, as of now, his brows were knotted, bearing the weight of his confusion, frustration, anger, and sadness.

He had closed a big case yesterday; he should have been happy. But, for some reason, he felt as though something was weighing him down.

Ashish loved only two things in the world, his job, and money. The latter meant so much to him, that he was ready to defend anyone who would give him the highest price. There were many times, when he would free a guilty man just for the sake of higher earnings. On these occasions when criminals approached him, Ashish would find himself in a conflict. But, eventually, the greed for wealth would win, and Ashish would end up convincing the judge to send an innocent man to jail.

Yesterday was such a day when Ashish had let a Russian hit man walk free, leaving a dead man's mother asking God what had become of humanity. Since then, wherever Ashish had gone, his blood-smeared conscience troubled him, first at the coffee shop, where he thought he found a bullet in the coffee, then at work, when his laptop had completely disintegrated in his hands, leaving him alone to hear the screams of the innocents pleading for justice, and now, when he found his house covered in blood.

"Is this what I have been reduced to? A man ready to help anybody, just for the sake of money. A man without morals?" Ashish thought. "A man ready to do injustice to an innocent person, just so that he can enjoy temporary, materialistic comforts? What happened to all my college days, where I took pride in the thought that one day, I would be fighting injustice and crime, the root of all evils?" Money had blinded him.

At that moment, Ashish finally woke up. To all the damage that he had done. He could not undo what he had done, but he could certainly change. The society was a rotten place with evils still pervading every sphere of life. He, Ashish, was going to put an end to all of that. He was going to cleanse society. In humanity's darkest hour, he would rise, a beacon of hope for all. He would free the society from those detested evils. He was going to be the saviour.

Ashish looked up, seeing the world through new eyes. Eyes which questioned every move of everyone he saw. They were nothing less than the eyes of blindfolded Justice. The tormented ghosts of his past tore at him and gnawed at his emptiness, but he found it strangely reassuring. He knew that, somehow or the other, he was now going to avenge them.

He vaguely remembered stepping into the kitchen and taking something from the drawer before he stepped onto the street, his sense of purpose fuelling him. But as he wandered onto the streets, his confidence began to diminish. It was such a huge world, with tons of people in it. He began doubting himself, wondering if it was possible to free society from evil itself. Evil, after all, was the other side of humanity, a second face, fused together and welded into society; the Mr Hyde of everyone's Dr Jekyll.

As soon as Ashish began doubting himself, his confidence began to falter, and his newfound hope fell victim to the anguished yells of the innocent. He began to lose purpose, and once again, succumbed to his negative thoughts. He ended up on the streets, attracting curious looks from the plainly clad people who looked at his crisp suit with curiosity.

He found himself at a metro station, and quickly bought himself a ticket to the other end of the city. It was a slack time of the day, and Ashish yearned for nothing more than some quiet time with his thoughts. The next thing he knew, he was seated in a pleasantly cool metro train, opposite to a venerable old man with a flowing, white beard. He smiled at Ashish, but Ashish paid no attention.

Ashish looked around and saw very few people seated in his compartment. He looked out of the window, at the lush, green pastures of paddy field which spread as far as the eyes could see. The fields gave way to factories creating the smoke which eventually mingled and became a part of society. As his feelings coursed through his body the world became blurry, and all Ashish could see was a multitude of bright colours through his teary eyes.

He wiped away the tears, wishing he could just as easily wipe away the screams of the unjustly accused from his soul. Ashish's inability to do anything frustrated him beyond measure, and he balled up his fists in anger to control himself from screaming out loudly.

Suddenly, the metro went dark.

There were whoops of laughter as the metro entered a tunnel, which turned into screams of terror as the lights in the cabin also went off, leaving them in pitch-darkness. People switched on the torch lights of their phones, enabling them to look around.

"Silence," said a commanding voice. By the light of the mobile-phone torches, Ashish could see the old man opposite to him stand up. "There is a bomb in the compartment." People gasped, looking at each other, not knowing how to respond.

"Society has reached a pathetic level. People should be living along with each other, not against each other. It's time we, the Gods from above, taught you humans a lesson, so that you learn to live with each other, and accept each other for who you are."

"A-a-and how you are going to do that?" asked a man, trembling.

The 'God' gazed into the man's eyes for a moment before taking a deep breath, pulling out a remote with a button and saying, "We're going to blow you sky-high."

Here it was, a God-sent opportunity for Ashish to prove his worth, to prove himself as the saviour. He was going to show the world that he was worthy, worthy of cleansing society. He was going to stop the man.

Carefully gripping the razor-sharp knife which had appeared into his back pocket, Ashish stood up like the others, trying not to make any suspicious movement. The old man looked at him and narrowed his brows. "What are you doing?"

"Me?" Ashish asked, trying to keep his voice from trembling. Then, suddenly, he lost his cool. "WHAT ARE YOU DOING? HOW CAN YOU THINK OF BLOWING UP A WHOLE TRAIN? SO MANY INNOCENTS WILL DIE, SO MANY…" Anger took over him, and he lost track of what he was saying.

He unsheathed his knife and advanced upon the old man, seeing visions of thrusting it into him after wrenching the remote out of the old man's hands. He could feel the people cheering him on, cheering on their protector. The old man's face twisted into an expression of fear, as he backed away from Ashish, yelling "WHAT HAVE I DONE? LEAVE ME ALONE! YOU'RE CRAZY!"

Ashish moved forward, saying coldly, "Blowing up a train? You're the one who is crazy. And I shall make you pay for endangering the lives of all these innocent people."

The muscles in Ashish's arm tautened, as he went in for the kill.   As soon as he thrust his arm forward, he was conscious of someone holding his arm back, protecting the old man. Ashish turned back, and saw a man gripping his arm tightly, looking at him, scared.

Suddenly, the darkness dissolved, and the world became fuzzy. Ashish fell to the ground, as the knife was snatched from him. He closed his eyes, breathing heavily. When he opened his eyes and looked around, a completely different environment greeted him. The lights on the metro were on, everyone was seated, and the old man was looking at Ashish, petrified.

Ashish buried his face in his hands, thinking, steadying his breath and his heart rate. "Did I imagine all of that?" he thought. "Did I hallucinate all of that just to prove myself worthy? What have I become?" Ashish inwardly screamed. He had never been so terrified of his own brain, of his own imagination, of his ability to weave stories, which would convince not only a jury, but even him!

The claustrophobic train was suffocating him, trapping him, imprisoning him. He had to break free. He rushed out onto the next platform before anybody could stop him and call the police. He had become a wild animal, running on the streets, trapped with his own thoughts, with his own imagination, searching for sanctuary, and for protection from the voices of the imprisoned souls.

Ashish ran helter-skelter trying to sort out the truth from the myriad visions. The more he thought about it, the more the happening of the weak made sense. The dragon, breathing down a torrent of fire from the heavens above, the lizards chasing him across the park, and Satan himself coming over to Ashish's birthday party and singing "Happy Death day to You", all of them were hallucinations, born out of a burdened mind.

Ashish ran to a park, hoping the lush greenery would soothe him. He sat down on a bench, and looked around, as a group of kids bounced a ball around, and a small girl fed breadcrumbs to a motley crew of birds. On the gravelled path, a group of runners jogged around the park, and the ducks in the pond quacked and splashed around joyfully, evading the remote-controlled boat.

Everything seemed peaceful, with life, laughter and simple joy in every moment. Ashish took a deep, calming breath, and reassured himself that everything would be okay. He looked up to the sky of endless possibilities and smiled to himself. He would get over the ghosts of his past. He would not let them torment him. He would start afresh. It would be the dawn of a new era.

As soon as he thought about this, his clear mind clouded over, and he could hear voices in his head, not just muffled muttering as he could hear before, but clear voices, as though they had finally tuned into his head.

"You let my killer walk free," said one, a hard, raspy voice. "Well, I shall never let you walk free. You shall always be burdened by your misdeeds, and the injustice you have done to others will weigh you down."

"Those who you love, and those who you have wronged, are people who will never truly leave you," said another, while others simply screamed in cacophony, giving Ashish a splitting headache.

He slipped onto the ground, clutching his forehead, as he rolled around the ground, battling the pain from within. "We will never leave youuuuuu," all the voices screamed, as Ashish began yelling out in pain. A gunman trained his gun from far away, smiling evilly. The children ran away from him, and the grown-ups ran towards him, trying to ease him back onto the bench and pour some water into his mouth.

Ashish felt his heart rate falter, as his blood flow dimmed. His eyesight blurred, and he could barely make out the cluster of voices which surrounded him. His heart rate slowed as the voices tore into his soul, shattering his character and unleashing raw agony. The last thing he remembered seeing was a number of people looking at him in concern, while someone called an ambulance. Then the sky turned dark, as his eyelids shut out the outside world.

* * * * *

Ashish soared through an endless, dark tunnel, reaching for the point-sized light from where he would exit the black tunnel of burden, and would become free. The light grew bigger and bigger and ultimately became a huge opening, leading him to the heavens above. He reached closer, yearning to reach that dimension of peace.

But, as soon as he reached the opening, something tugged him, as though there was an invisible fishing-rod hooked around his navel. It was thraldom to those unjustly punished souls, and to those whose death had been rendered restless due to Ashish.

He had to head back, head back to the world of pain and sorrow, where he had to right his wrongs. He had to send the guilty to the gallows and had to free the innocent who had been unjustly penalized.

After a huge battle of his yearning for peace and his conscience, he turned with a huge sigh. He soared back through the endless tunnel, this time, to be reunited with himself.

* * * * *

The doctors swarmed around the man lying on the bed, pumping sedatives and saline, as he hovered between life and death. The electrocardiograph showed an erratic pulse, as the comatose man lay still as a stick in bed.

The man had collapsed in a park, for reasons unknown, and for two weeks, doctors had tried their best to bring him back to consciousness. The nurses rushed here and there, carrying out tests and bringing reports. And then, all of a sudden, the man's pulse steadied, and he began to breathe normally. His hands began to move, and he began squinting at the bright light shining down on him.

A few moments later, his eyelids fluttered open, and he said weakly, "I'm back from my prison."

He was ready for the case.

UPLIFTING FALL

Pratima Jaidev

Thud! .....I woke up all of a sudden and found myself lying on the floor next to my cot. I was profusely sweating, my heart beat was intense, my lips were dry, and I almost forgot for a moment why I was on the floor. Was it an anxiety attack? Was it a bad dream or did my blood pressure just drop? I heard mom's voice from a distance, "Samyu, see, you fell down again! You don't take my words seriously. I have told you several times to sleep straight on the cot and not to turn around a lot."

Mom's words took me back to my first day of the film school after my twelfth grade. Just after a month of joining the school, I sprained my back by lifting heavy buckets of water to third floor of my hostel due to the water shortage in that city. My hostel warden and my best friend, Bindi, took me to a local doctor, got the necessary tests done, and I was advised bed rest for three months. So, I had to pack my bags and get back home until I recovered completely.

At home, my overprotective mom did everything she could to keep her notorious teenage daughter engaged throughout the day so that I don't complain about lying down on the hard mattress the entire day without moving. She moved my cot to the living room, and I was allowed to watch TV for long hours as compensation for not riding my bike. I watched the movies I loved on the rented DVDs, and she bought me my favourite novels to read as well. She also ensured that I got my share of entertainment from time to time by inviting guests home who would keep me engaged in discussions about films, and they also used to play board games with me. Mom was never tired of making extra food for these guests who helped me forget my pain. Everybody just loved her food, and I guess, she has now passed on her culinary skills to me and my sister Goosy (my nickname for her).

Dad used to join us for dinner, and it became our routine to discuss all the movies that I binge watched during the day. The couch around my cot became our make-shift dining area for as long as I was restricted to the bed. Our menu for dinner always used to be of my choice, and sometimes I used to choose dishes which both Goosy and I liked so that she doesn't complain.

Dad always allowed Goosy and me to discuss even the censored version of topics like young girls wearing short clothes, our male classmates flirting and following us home etc. Mom initially was not open to the fact that we were discussing everything with dad. But, she realized that it is better for us to discuss with both of them so that we learn to handle situations confidently, unlike, few of my friends who fell prey to dangerous circumstances like boys threatening them with acid attacks if their love proposals were not accepted, getting bullied or slut shamed in school and resulting in health problems like anorexia, bulimia, depression etc. Mom wanted both her daughters to develop good inter-personal skills while being careful with the relationships we form. She once asked an Anglo Indian guy in my apartment to teach me 'to ride a bicycle' for which she had to face a lot of criticism from all other women in my apartment complex. But, she paid a deaf ear to everything as she was confident that we would never misuse the freedom that we had.

When the long day ended, the only thing which remained fresh was mom's innocent smile and her hearty laugh. While retiring to bed, her major task was to ensure that I do not fall off the bed. So, she used to sleep next to me on the same cot which was enough only for one person. How uncomfortable it must have been? I wonder today -how many times she must have woken up, only to prevent herself from falling and then to squeeze herself back on the cot just to ensure that I don't twist my waist.

With mom's strict regiment, I was up and running in a month and a half, earlier than the recovery time mentioned by the doctor. Her joy knew no bounds. But, I had to discontinue my course at the film institute and take a break of one year from education to recover completely. I knew mom would stand by me and support my decision of going to the U.S. for my film studies, and so she did. She convinced dad and reminded him of the promise he had made to me when he discontinued my studies after my fall.

Today, if I have successfully completed my Masters in Film studies from a prestigious university in the U.S.A, won a 'Best Director' trophy for one of my short films, a trophy for working as 'Best Associate' for an International Award winning project, and received critical acclaim at my workplace(s) across various industry verticals in 17 years of my career so far; it has all been possible only because of mom's confidence in me. Every hurdle that I have now crossed, involved their equal share of risks, struggle, and a lot of hard work. It was mom's pep talk, her strong belief in her upbringing, and her constant support that made all my achievements possible.

Both mom and dad have always taught me and Goosy to aim high, take calculated risks, face life's challenging situations boldly, and always have a positive approach to any and every situation that we come across in life.

While I walked down the memory lane of my teenage days, I suddenly felt very thirsty and realized that I was still sitting on the floor. The clock struck 12:00 at midnight. I got up from the floor and went to drink some water from the refrigerator. On my way back to my room, I saw mom's photograph hanging in the living room with a garland. Oh my god! I realized one more time that she left us four years ago. Why did mom suddenly appear in my dream, wake me up with a fall, and remind me of my back pain episode which I hated the most in my life? What was she trying to communicate?

Was mom trying to tell me that I have to move on in life irrespective of every fall that I come across? And, that I should be focusing on my career and taking care of my health that has been drastically failing from the past few months? I think mom has been listening from above to all my friends who are complaining about my constant weight loss.

Mom always wanted both her daughters to be independent and not to be confined to home like her. She wanted all her sacrifices and her unfulfilled dreams to be fruitful for us. I think it's time for me to get back into action and that's what she tried to communicate to me as I was drifting away from life , engulfed by depression, lost all my connections with the outside world and was moving at a snail's pace which doesn't match that of everyone around me.

I then looked at the calendar. It was 'Mother's day!' That reminds me of mom's 'never-give-up' attitude for 20 long years – as she battled with multiple health conditions apart from being a patient of 'Chronic Kidney Disorder.' Her attitude has only instilled faith in me time, and again and it has constantly reminded me of my duties towards my family as well as my profession.

During her last days, she had hallucinations of leaving us soon. Though she had a lot of difficulty with her day-to-day activities; her will was undeterred to survive only to provide moral support for her family. This attitude of hers has provided me with unflinching support to stay grounded and remain strong during challenging situations that life has thrown at me, ever since she left us.

Mom used to hide from us, all her pain from the several surgeries that she underwent and also the pain from dialysis with a hearty smile. It was her smile alone which has made us believe strongly in one thing – "No problem in life is as big as one's life itself." Mom taught us that the best way to face any conflicting situation in life, is to face it with a smile. Mom's smile is what kept me going when I was bedridden, it was her smile and "Nothing Is Impossible" attitude which enabled dad to tackle demanding clients and take tough business decisions while also carving a future for many youngsters who joined his company. Again, it's her smile which enabled Goosy to confidently crack all her competitive exams and qualify as a doctor.

Mom, "it is amazing how one fall of mine has refreshed your Samyu's memory of the numerous falls that you had for me and for the entire family." I take this as your signal from above that you will continue to guide us in all our endeavours and help us move on with the enriched life that you have given us.

"Love you mom!"

"Happy Mother's Day!"

"You are the best mom ever!"

"Goosy and I will try our best to live up to your expectations!!!"

WHO, WHERE, WHY, WHAT IS HE?

Ravi Gowri Theja

"I can't see you work so hard for a one-hour event, ma," the frustration in my voice sounded low and solid.

"That's okay. Now, go and get ready. Here, take this… you have a lot of work to do after you get ready. So, try to be as fast as you can… your uncle is working alone. He needs your assistance," my mother handed me the cotton dhoti as I watched my father with a raging look.

"Don't take him serious. You know how tensed your father is, and your uncle can't work without us. We must help him… this is normal for us," my mother said out of anguish and pushed me towards bathroom.

The plain dhoti was a bit rough and smelled like a new one. I locked my room and took a couple of minutes to calm myself down. My eyes were burning as I fit an LED focusing light in the living room a couple of minutes back. My fingers moved involuntarily and rubbed my eyes. The smell of the raw and sticky chrysanthemum essence filled my nostrils. The smell must have lingered on my hands when I was tying the festoon on the doors and the railing of the stairs. It wasn't just chrysanthemum; it was mixed with fresh turmeric.

Is it necessary to do these things for the sake of just one hour? All we are doing is a time-pass act of foolishness in the name of God. Waste of money, energy and everybody's time. Do this to keep the bad away from you, do that to make your God happy, wear this colour, eat without onions and garlic, starve for a day without drinking water, decorate your home with flowers and leaves etc. etc. etc. If you oppose them by raising valid points, they use their trump card: see it as Science, art and discipline. I kicked my bed in frustration until I realized my eyes were moist.

I believe in Community Service since my schooling. My father, the great Meenakshi Surendra Sharma, the head of the organization, which carries a certain religious activity throughout a month every year. All the members in the organization get together at a place and praise God in chanting in Sanskrit. Every day, at a different place, mostly at members' homes. Today, it was at our home and the estimation was that around 180 would attend.

Just imagine, all 180 members shouting together at a time harmoniously! The suffocation they create inside a closed room, the noise of *bhajans* and claps, they leave slippers before entering the house and then playing football later to find them, throwing the paper cups and plates in which *Panchamrutha* and food would be served. It would also be likely that the floor turns sticky because of people spilling *teertham* and *prasadam* while they eat and drink.

How can I tell them, 'Your god never listens to what you shout'...?

How can I tell them, 'Learn and try to understand what you are saying... do not make your ignorance drive your innocence... that's how you'll get to know the truth behind what you say or do'?

At least, 'go and do some useful work.'

With all these thoughts spiralling in my mind, I wore my dhoti and a plain white T-shirt and stepped out of my room. My father was running across the living room in tension. My uncle, grandmother, aunt and a family friend were arranging the stage and lighting. I stepped out to find the chairs that I ordered for rent.

"Yetheish... go and bring a garland. It's urgent! I only brought two and now realized that we need a third one. Please go and bring," my father came out and pleaded me.

I looked at him as if I hate him the most on this earth. That was what I felt at that moment. I spoke nothing and took the money from his hand and dragged the stuck bike out of the wet mud outside the house.

Has he gone mad? Why is he wasting so much of money for just one hour? And why is mother saying okay to all this madness? While driving, I questioned to the character called 'my father' that was framed inside my head as if he had answers to all my questions.

I brought the garland and handed it to him. He took it from me and smiled.

"Yetheish, you stay here until it gets finished inside," my father said.

As if I would've sat along with you even after you plead me, I thought and turned my face away from him.

I had no problem if he had donated all the money to orphanages, old-age homes or feeding the needy. Everybody who would be attending today got enough money and ate well all three times every day. Most of them are government officers, retired officers, and businessmen who collectively waste time by attending these meetings in the name of Dharma.

Giving them return gifts, fruits, *prasadam*, all that waste. With that money, we can feed many poor people. And all can feed… I don't know! I can only hate myself for being here and watching this nonsense.

People started appearing in front of the opened gate and awaited someone's presence there. I stood up and started greeting them by folding my hands with a smile and courtesy - the first lesson I learned from my mother when I was a kid.

As expected, slippers and other kinds of footwear were thrown aside unaware of the confused football match that they gonna play before leaving. Almost 23 members entered the house at once.

These people who are obsessed with God, no matter how many events they attend, this is how they remove their footwear and create the first step of mess, I thought and involuntarily moved towards the place.

I started picking them with my hands and arranged them in serial rows in an order. Looking at me picking up the slippers and arranging them properly, some people left their shoe-wear properly and touched my head with their hands. Ignoring their gesture, I focused on my job of setting them.

They started shouting the Sanskrit shlokas inside. People started to flow in from all directions.

Oldies in the group murmured about me. All I heard was 'Surendra's son is picking them with hands…'

At least now you realize how undisciplined and un-orderly your ways are, old men, I thought.

An old woman with thick-glass spectacles who just entered looked at me. I looked at her. Her eyes seemed larger than their size through her specs. Her grey, messy, and curly hair was tied with a black rubber band. She held my arm with her delicate old hand and started leaving her footwear. I held back tightly by providing her extra support.

I knew her from a local hotel where she washes bowls, dishes and plates. My parents used to send me there on every Sunday morning to have a masala dosa. I knew her since I was a child or since she worked in that hotel whichever was earlier.

She smiled at me and pinched my cheeks and said, "thank you, Kannan! I still remember you, standing in the queue awaiting order. I'm so happy to see you becoming a fine man."

"*Avva*, thank you. Hope your health is good," I inquired. She smiled again and entered the house.

How is she able to learn those difficult Sanskrit phrases and shlokas. I wondered, though it sounded like I judged her.

My father folded his hands and invited her into the house with a beaming smile.

'Oh! Look at him... he received her well...' I thought. At first, my instinct told me that he is going to ignore her presence and treat her like the same serving old woman, but he acted in a quite opposite way.

Happy to see you like this, Mr. Meenakshi Surendra Sharma, I appreciated him with a lovely sarcasm.

A middle-aged man entered with his mentally challenged son. My expression was very warm and calm. Next moment, I knelt and I opened my arms to embrace the little lad. He constantly moved his head, but his vision was fixed.

He hugged me and tapped on my head, like an elderly man. I chuckled at his way of expression through a hug. His father smiled and left his footwear, and I continued to pick them and arrange in an order.

"No, no, no, stop doing this!" one of my father's friends held my hand and stopped me from picking the slippers.

'What the... what happened?'

"Uncle! It is fine... I have no problem in doing this," I said with an uneasy smile. I hate to see them play football so, I am only trying to help them to find their slippers easily.

"You are a Brahmin. You shouldn't do this... who told you to do so?" He started shouting at me.

'Oh no! Stop pointing me as a Brahmin. I do what I need to do and that makes me feel happy... stop being stereotypical...' I thought.

"I'm trying to help them, uncle. After today, they shall put theirs in an order, I'm trying to remind them by doing this," I tried to convince him.

"They should learn it. You don't make your hands dirty for them, Yetheish," he said and shook my hand to leave the slippers.

"Maybe... change starts from us, uncle. This is how I've been raised... I don't have any problem in doing this," I replied by rising my tone. In the meanwhile, my father came out and found me arguing.

"Surendra... look at your son. He is picking slippers with hands and putting them in order," uncle complained to my father.

"Leave him *Appa*, he won't listen. He can't resist untidy and disorderly surroundings," my father said to his friend and grabbed his hand.

"Xerox copy... you should make your children learn about good things but not these things," he replied as if I did something wrong. My father smiled at me and took his friend inside. He turned back to find me not picking the slippers, but I am holding his shoes that he left aside.

After their chants completed, the main scene arrived. *Panchamrutha* and *prasadam*.

I'm not here to entertain your freedom of throwing glasses and paper plates everywhere; I thought and rushed inside to get a bin.

Before I came with the bin, the humans, who came after the godly service had started throwing the glasses in the corner.

I put the bin in front of the gate and this time, I picked the glasses from the corner and dumped in the bin.

My father came and stood beside me. He started shaking his hands with the people who attended the ceremony today.

"How did it go?" Father asked me.

I ignored his question and kept myself busy with the people around.

"You are the star of today's event, Yethish! Good job," he said.

"I'm doing my job. I didn't do so that people praise me or for your god or for you," I replied. He laughed softly.

"The old woman you greeted earlier; people won't acknowledge/treat her with respect because she works in a hotel that too as a servant. You spoke to her and held her. You see! A small gesture of recognizing made her to sit in the first row. What did you see in this?" He asked in a low voice.

"Tell me the answer. Don't pause," I said putting my irritation along with my words.

"People aren't like you, Yetheish. They discriminate a person till they are acknowledged. You are an exception who treats everybody as equal," he said while shaking his hands with others.

"The mentally-challenged boy whom you hugged earlier… people used to shout at him for his ear-splitting chanting of shlokas," he said.

'Oh! Mr. Meenakshi Surendra Sharma is speaking now...' I thought.

"Today I didn't see anyone yelling at him or closing his mouth. As you saw him like a beautiful thing before he entered, they started looking at him as a human. For the first time, they appreciated his little devotion. People don't see the inner beauty till it gets exposed," he said.

"He is acting wise...' I thought. This time, my heart started responding.

"Today's biggest act... putting slippers in an order!" He exclaimed.

"No matter how well-educated you are or which family you belong to... bow down to earth and greet people with respect," He showed his real face.

'Is that so? Such a deep meaning...' my brain totally got covered by his logic.

"Finally, my dear Yetheish! I didn't do this for God-sake. But I did this to show how my son works without feeling proud or shy. Because he is the Xerox copy of Meenakshi Surendra Sharma..."

BALLERINA WHO WORE GLASSES

Ruchi Shrivastava

MEERA, THE INVENTOR

Meera felt Nitya pushing her away with her elbow.

"Just that last line, silly," Meera muttered, still bent over Nitya's notebook with her short blunt hair falling over the notebook.

"Miss Roy is here," Nitya whispered, still nudging her away.

"Oh!" Meera lifted her head with her face covered with hair. She parted it apart with little fingers and sneaked through the hair strands.

Two big eyes peeped out of the round glasses, a red round bindi, and smell of jasmine flowers.

It must be Miss Roy, Meera muttered.

"Stop peeping and answer the last equation," Miss Roy asked loudly to Meera and pointed towards the blackboard.

Meera squinted at the blackboard and replied feebly, "answer is 123."

"Wrong. The answer is 4," Miss Roy scolded back.

It was not that Meera was not good at math, it was just that she could not see the blackboard very well. Meera knew that she had an eye problem, but never wanted to share with anyone.

"Wish I had a sensor watch," Meera sighed.

"And what would that do?" Nitya raised her eyebrows.

"Sensor Watch could sense Miss Singh was here and alarm me," the thought of a new discovery made Meera's eyes twinkle.

Sensor Watch, invention no. 14 added to the master list.

Tiiirrrgggggg. The bell rang, and it was lunchtime.

Meera rolled and stuffed the whole chapati in her mouth and leaped out of the classroom. Wasting even a single minute of the lunch break was crime.

She ran as fast as she could towards the playground. If you miss reaching the playground in time, then you miss finding a spot for yourself, and all you do is stand aside and watch others play.

Dhammaaaaalll!!

"You did not see the string, silly," Nitya giggled, she held Meera's hand to help her get up.

The school was preparing for the Sports Day. Fresh white marks were put for the race ground. The ground was under the 'DO NOT ENTER' zone and so a string was tied to restrict children from spoiling the marks.

"What a mess," Meera grumbled at the string as she dusted her skirt.

"Why don't you tell Amma about your eye problem?" Nitya knew about Meera's eye problem but had been an honest friend to not confess to anyone.

"Because, they would make me wear glasses," replied Meera

"But glasses look cool," Nitya chuckled. Nitya had always wished to wear glasses. Last time, she made a false complaint of eye problem and visited the doctor, but the doctor confirmed that her eyesight was fine.

And another time she made her own glasses with straws. They made her look cool until her cat Jenny chewed them up.

"Cool??" Meera crimped her nose, "Glasses look dumb."

"Have you ever seen a ballerina with glasses?" Meera threw a valid case point as she twirled inside the playground.

"They could make a siren string," Meera rushed and grabbed a spot for her and Nitya to play hopscotch.

"And what would that do?" Nitya asked, throwing her stone inside the first square.

"So, whenever you come closer to trespassing such strings, it would sense and make noise." "Meera the Inventor" chuckled.

"Siren String", invention No.15 added to the master list.

Meera had two dreams.

A- Inventions. When she grows up, she wants to invent and build things which would ease other's lives and solve a purpose. She started with her master list when she was just five! The first item in the invention list was 'Face Helmet' for cooking. She had seen Amma getting hurt while tempering the curry.

B- Ballet.

*****

I CAN SEE FINE

Later that evening on her way back home, Meera saw Amma anxiously taking rounds in the balcony. She instantly knew something is definitely wrong, because every time when something was not right, Amma took too many rounds in the balcony. This might be her idea to reduce her tension, or her weight, or both!

Appa is home early today.

"What?" she asked looking at the worried face of Amma.

"1 or 2?" Amma asked, raising her fingers.

Meera threw her school bag on the sofa, raised her eyebrows, and put her hands on her hip.

"That is silly. I can see fine!"

"Can you read this," Appa asked pointing to the calendar on the wall.

Meera squinted her eyes hard, but no, she could not read a word.

Reading anything from a distance was difficult for Meera. The alphabets appeared like small ants standing in a queue.

"Can you tell me what you see there?" asked Noel, pointing to the brown cat sitting on their house railing. Noel is Meera's younger brother but often acts as an elder one.

"Shut up, don't try to be over smart," Meera scolded him back.

"You need a check-up, dear. We will go to the doctor tomorrow," Amma confirmed and went back to the kitchen.

"I can see fine," Meera announced and went straight to her room.

Miss Roy, her class teacher, called Amma and informed her about Meera always squinting her eyes and peeping into other children's notebook.

"She would always peep into Nitya's notebook to copy the text. You should get her eyes checked," Miss Roy said to Amma.

Even the tuition teacher had also complained that Meera would always squint her eyes to read from the notebook.

That evening Meera finished her dinner early and went straight to bed. She was in no mood to listen to Amma's bedtime story or play with Noel. She pulled up the sheet up to her face and closed her eyes tightly, but in no way, she could sleep tonight.

Amma was taking her for an eye test and that scared her.

"What would happen tomorrow?" "Will the doctor give her glasses?" "How will she look in the glasses?" "How will she dance with the glasses?"

Too many questions came bouncing to Meera's head but not even one answer.

*****

THE EYE TEST

Next morning Meera and Amma got ready to visit the ophthalmologist. This was one of the few journeys where she was not enjoying the bus ride, otherwise bus rides were her favourite. Looking out of the window to observe people hopping in and out at the stops, the trees moving swiftly from the window view, and her favourite was the ticket man in khaki. The rickety sound he made when he punched the ticket was exciting to Meera.

They arrived on time to the hospital. The hospital was a huge building with multiple blocks. The watchman at the gate looked at her and asked them to walk to Block B.

"Why do all watchmen have such grinning faces?" Meera grinned back at the watchman. Even the watchman at her school, Nandu kaka had a grinning face. He kept an eagle eye on each one and knew every child by name.

"3rd Floor, please," said the lady at the reception of Block B.

They went near the lift. After a minute of waiting, the lift came down. And a rush of people came out from the lift.

So many people with eye problems! Meera's thought was interrupted by a push from a wheelchair.

A little boy was sitting on the wheelchair. His both eyes were covered with a white bandage. The helper staff helped him come out of the lift.

"What did they do with his eyes?" That thought itself gave Meera a shiver down her spine.

Amma pulled her inside the lift. The lift was full of patients. She tightly held the edge of Amma's saree pallu.

The lift stopped at the 3rd floor which was the children's section.

"This way to the left," another lady staff directed them to the waiting area.

Waiting hall was huge with rows of sitting chairs. There were small windows all around. There was a play area section too, with a slide, a toy house, and a red seesaw. Meera and Amma took their seats in the third row.

The waiting hall was full of children who had come for the checkup.

"Oh! How they look with the glasses," "How do they play with those big glasses," "Do they sleep with those," since last evening Meera did not have a moment of peace. Zillions of questions bounced in her head but again, answer to none.

"Meera Sharma, next turn. Room no. 4," her name was called out.

The doctor helped them to the check-up room.

It was a small room with pink walls. There was a whiteboard on one wall and a small television on the side wall.

Meera sat on the highchair.

"Stop that. Sit still," Amma was annoyed looking at her as she swung her legs in the air.

Dhaamm Dhaaaam!! Meera's heart thumped like a drum.

"What is going to happen next," the thought made her shiver.

Suddenly Meera felt hot and fizzy. Her ears buzzed. The room walls seemed to come closer. She wanted to reach out to Amma until the door opened and made a racket noise.

"Hey, you little birdie," "What happened," the young doctor made the environment comfortable with her pleasant smile.

"I can see fine," Meera muttered feebly.

"Aww...do not worry. We will check that," the doctor chimed in.

The doctor put a heavy metal frame on her eyes. That was heavy. She felt like a character from Star Wars who wore a spooky gadget.

"Circle or square?" The Doctor asked pointing towards the board.

"Square," how lame, she could see the big square very clearly.

"Read the alphabets, Meera."

"L M O X….P.. no.. R..no no B", Meera tried to squint her eyes hard to read the last line but got messed up.

"Look up."

"Look down."

"Right."

"Left," the Doctor was moving the torch swiftly in all directions.

"Is everything ok? Does she need glasses?" Amma asked the doctor. She had been worried all day.

Meera had heard Amma talking to Appa last night.

`How did this happen? She would have to wear glasses at such an early age. She looks so pretty now. How will she grow with those?' Amma was almost in tears and Appa was consoling her.

Amma had never been too self-conscious about her own looks. Her maximum makeup look consisted of the red round *bindi* and dark *kajal.* But today Amma was conscious about how Meera would look in the glasses.

"Yes, there is a slight vision problem. She needs glasses," the doctor confirmed.

Amma was devastated.

"Oh," is all she could say, as she sulked the lump in her throat.

"If you wear them enough you might grow out of them in a few years," the doctor said squishing Meera's cheeks.

Meera's heart sank.

"Glasses!!"

Her face drooped like a wilted flower.

The doctor came closer and said to Meera, "You have a new friend, your glasses. They are for you and you are for them."

* * * * *

MEERA'S NEW FRIEND

With the prescription in one hand, Meera and Amma went down to the ground floor of the hospital to choose Meera's new friend, her glasses!

"Wow, don't they really look cool?" Amma screamed with a weird over enthusiastic tone pointing to the poster of kids with glasses.

Meera was in no interest to look at those posters. She knew she was going to look dumb and everyone would make fun of her.

They went inside a small shop filled with glasses. Meera looked around, Glasses Everywhere!

On the walls.

On the table.

On the shelves.

On the posters...Everywhere!!

Oval, Square, Rectangle, Circle...All Shapes!!

Red, Black, Brown and Beige...All Colours!!

She looked up at the ceiling fan. Her head spun like one.

Soon began the process of choosing the 'Perfect one'.

Amma picked up the brown round ones.

"No," nodded Meera.

The helper suggested black rectangular one.

Meera crimped her nose.

Maroon with a thin frame...too nerdy.

Brown-winged...yuck!!

Star-shaped...how kiddish!

The one with strings....no way!

Amma and the helper tried almost all the frames available in the shop, but no one seemed to impress Meera.

Or was she trying that choosing none would skip her chance of wearing one.

Finally, the helper picked the last one in the third row, the round metal circular frame with a subtle of a pink shade.

It sat perfectly on Meera's nose like a crown sits on the princess' head.

'You look so pretty,' Amma seemed excited but Meera gave her usual un-bothered look.

They had to wait for some time until the staff returned with the glasses fixed to the frame as per the prescription.

'Try on,' the staff slid the glasses on Meera.

'I really don't need these. I can see fi--.' the thin crisp line of Amma's red *bindi* cut her before she could complete the sentence.

She turned left and read, 'Buy 1 Get 1,' the crisp lines of alphabets made her aghast.

She turned right to the mirror, 'Is that me? Ridiculous!'

'I don't want them Amma,' Meera said twitching her nose to adjust the glasses.

Meera got a new friend. It was a round metal circular frame.

*****

THE NOT SO GOOD FRIEND

Next morning Meera was ready for school. She went to Amma's room and stood up on the stool to look at herself in the mirror. This is her every day morning routine.

Neatly done hair with a black headband, white collared shirt, pleated blue skirt, socks pulled up to the knee and her shining black shoes.

But today she looked different. She is now 'the girl with the glasses.'

The metal circular frame sat on her tiny little nose.

"I don't like you," Meera mumbled as she twitched and twisted her nose.

Amma had made *upma* for breakfast. Amma always made the most delicious tomato *upma*.

Meera couldn't stop her self-indulging in the aroma of hot red tomato *upma*. But, suddenly the *upma* seemed blurred. The steam from hot *upma* got over the glasses.

"I don't like you," Meera mumbled putting away her glasses on the table.

Meera was ready to leave. She picked up her bag, lunch box, and umbrella.

"You must wear them all the time," Amma said, passing the glasses to Meera.

Her school was close to her home. Everyday Meera and Jai walk together to the school.

Meera and Jai studied in the same school and in the same class. Even their fathers worked in the same office. Their mothers too were good friends. Jina aunty would come to their home to have the evening cup of tea together.

Jai was a favourite boy in her home. Everybody loved him. He would help Amma get the coriander from the nearby shop. Even Appa called him while cleaning the cycle. Noel too was friendly to him. One time he saved Noel from slipping down from the balcony. How everybody was all praises for Jai!

He is just so good at everything.

But Meera did not like Jai much. She thought that he is bossy with her and always corrected her.

Amma would always ask Meera to go and study with Jai.

"Why Amma? I can study by myself."

"Because he comes first in class. Go and revise with him. Look how neatly he prepares his notes."

Today, she was a bit nervous about Jai. What would he say about her glasses? Would he make fun of her?

"Hey, you got glasses," Jai asked Meera looking at her glasses.

"Yes"

"Cool," was all he said.

No further list of questions came from him. It looked like an ordinary issue to him. Meera was relieved.

Suddenly it started to drizzle. Meera loved rain. She lifted her head up to let the raindrops fall on her face.

But again, the sky blurred and everything around became hazy. The fresh big raindrops slipped down her glasses and made it difficult for her to view anything.

"I don't like you. You will never be my friend," Meera mumbled again keeping her glasses in her pocket.

Why don't glasses come with wipers? A very weird and valid invention struck her.

"Glasses with Wipers," invention no.16 added to her master list.

And for all these reasons, Meera did not like her new glasses. More than solving her problem, the glasses were creating more.

*****

MEERA GOT A NEW NAME

Roll no. 23, Miss Roy called names for attendance.

"Present Ma'am," Meera raised her hands up.

Miss Roy lifted her head up and looked through her round glasses, "Meera, why are you not wearing your glasses? Your mom called me and told me about your eye test. You must always wear it."

All heads in the class turned towards Meera. She reluctantly took the glasses from the pocket and put it over.

"You did not tell me about it," Nitya poked her with a pencil.

As soon the attendance got over and Miss Roy left the classroom, everyone gathered around Meera's desk.

It seemed the class discovered the ninth wonder!

"Discoverer Meera is now Defective Meera," Monty chuckled and the whole class burst into laughter.

Suddenly Monty came forward and snatched Meera's glasses and started to run all over the class.

Meera ran after him but could not catch him. She kept asking to return it back, but Monty kept annoying her shouting back, nana at her.

Nitya caught him and pushed him back.

"You look cute piggy," Nitya smiled and handed over the glasses to Meera.

Soon, Miss Singh, the English teacher was in class, and everyone ran to their desk and settled down.

Miss Singh started to write on the blackboard. Suddenly Miss Singh turned back and looked at Meera, "Meera can you read it," she asked.

Meera stood up adjusting her glasses and said, "Yes Ma'am."

"Defective Meera," Monty chuckled again.

Meera groaned back to him.

*****

Later that evening, Meera flung the school bag on the table and bounced on the sofa.

"I will get your favourite chocolate shake," Amma knew that Meera did not have a very good day at school.

Just then, Jina aunty came in for her usual cup of tea.

"Is that for real," Jina aunty almost screamed seeing Meera's glasses.

"No, they are just imaginary, and I can also do some magic with that!" Meera muttered rolling her eyes at Jina aunty.

"What's wrong with her eyes?" Jina Aunty went straight to the kitchen

"It is totally reasonable to ask why someone is wearing glasses, but it is silly to ask what's wrong with the eyes, Meera wanted to shout back at Jina aunty, but Amma always told her to behave well in front of elders, especially Jina aunty.

"Poor baby," Jina Aunty threw her favourite sympathy liner.

"Yes, wearing glasses is difficult but there is nothing to be sympathetic about it. It helps to see clearly and does not require pity."

"But she looks cute in those," another sympathy liner.

"That sounds nice to hear, but it is hurtful at the same time. It sounds like we did not look cute without them, and that's simply not true."

Meera slurped her chocolate shake louder. But she could still hear the noise from the kitchen.

"Give her more spinach soup."

"Reduce the tv time."

"Blah...Blah!"

Meera went inside her room and shut the door. No noise.

Sluurrrpppp!!

Amma made the most tasty chocolate shake.

* * * * *

THE NOT-SO GOOD SPORTS DAY

Today was the first day of school fest. Every year the school held a three-day fest called 'Eureka'.

Day1: Sports Day. This year Meera was participating in the high jump.

Day2: Cultural

Day3: Closing Ceremony, which was all about fun and food.

Mr. Singh, her PT teacher said that she could win the event. She jumps the highest.

Meera had been practicing a lot for her jump. One afternoon she tried to jump from her bed to Noel's bed but badly fell.

"Meera, stop behaving like a monkey," Amma yelled from the kitchen and Noel giggled.

How can Amma see everything even when she is not around? She must be having some superpower.

And why do these younger brothers are such monkeys?

Soon, everybody gathered around the event area. Mr. Singh was adjusting the bar, checking the sand and re-doing the white marks.

Jai was also participating in this event.

"You can win today," Nitya chucked. "This is your chance to beat Jai".

Meera was all smiles. Yes, this was her day to become the new favorite.

Mr. Singh asked all the participants to stand in a queue.

Mr. Singh blew the whistle and the event was declared open. He started to call out the names one by one.

Standing behind Nitya, suddenly Meera felt restless. She started to sweat. Her heart started to thump loudly. There was a buzzing sound all over and the field seemed to be moving up and down.

The biggest question of her life crept in from inside her tummy…

"What shall I do with the glasses?"

"Should I run with them or without them?" Before she could ask Nitya for help, Nitya had already started her run.

"Remove them. You can see fine," the heart argued.

"But how will you see the mark," the mind corrected.

"Meera, next turn," Mr. Singh called her name.

Almost everyone had performed their jump. Up until now, Jai's jump was the highest recorded.

Everything was on Meera. She can perform the jump of her life and win the game. She would become the star of the school and everyone's new favorite.

1...2...3...whistle. Mr. Singh gave the signal.

Meera removed the glasses and put it in her pocket.

She ran as fast as she could.

She leaped like a mighty tigress. As she reached the white mark, she pushed herself high, very high. Her whole body flung in the air.

Everybody around watched Meera take the jump with their eyes wide open and breath out.

But all they could hear was a thump... a loud thump.

Dhaaapaaaaak!

The glasses fell out from her pocket.

Meera got hit by the rod and fell like a kitten from the tree.

The children giggled.

Mr. Singh rolled his eyes. Meera could not even make a successful jump. She was disqualified.

Nitya's face wilted like a dry flower and Jai's shone like the sun.

Meera collected herself and got up. She herself was surprised by what had happened.

While she ran and took leaps like a tigress, she missed seeing the mark and made the wrong jump before the mark and got hit by the rod.

She had lost.

Her heart wanted to burst out. She wanted to cry loud and high. Two big tears rolled down her eyes.

Mr. Singh was congratulating Jai on his win.

Everything around became blurry again. She ran away from the crowd. She wanted to run away from the whole world. She could hear Nitya calling from behind, but she did not stop. She felt like a loser.

She ran to the water tap station and felt like dipping her head in the chilled cold water. She cried loudly and high. Nobody was there to hear.

"All this happened because of you."

"I hate you," she yelled at the glasses throwing it away on the ground.

"You can never be my friend."

* * * * *

MISS BALLERINA IS BETTER THAN MISS FALLERINA

"Not today Amma," Meera took a step back as she saw Amma standing near the door with her glasses in hand.

Meera's second dream is ballet.

Amma had enrolled her at a very early age. Even for her first birthday, Amma dressed her as a ballerina. Pink tutu skirt, pink headband, and pink pointe shoes.

The other day she was very happy when Miss Sangeeta, the dance teacher announced that this year the school will be performing a ballet dance for Eureka fest.

"Wow," a chance to twirl and swirl on the school stage. What else could she have asked for?

She was the first one to get selected for the group performance, Miss Sangeeta even asked her to help Joyce and Meena.

Back home, she flung the school bag on the sofa and ran to the terrace.

"Amma, we are performing ballet for Eureka. One day you will be the proud mother of India's finest ballerina."

Amma nodded her head in encouragement.

Meera opened her arms and twirled on toes and

Bhaaaammmmm!!

The pickle jar fell off.

"You must wear your glasses Miss Ballerina, or else you could become Miss Fallerina," Amma teased her.

Next morning, Meera was up early. She just could not wait for the day to start. She dressed up and went straight to Amma's room. She stood on the stool to look at herself. She could not stop boasting about herself. Suddenly, all the excitement seemed to melt.

"Ballerina's don't wear glasses," Meera grumbled and sat on the bed as she saw Amma holding the glasses.

It was a valid point. Nobody had ever seen a ballerina with glasses.

"They probably might be wearing contact lenses, and you can get them when you are older enough," Amma said as she tightly made the bun.

"But I will not look pretty," Meera was reluctant as it might reduce her perfect ballerina look.

"You will look beautiful, my flower child. It is the shine of one's confidence that completes a dancer's beauty," Amma put her arms around her.

"What if judges deduct marks?" Meera put her another case.

"Why would they?"

"Your group has excellent technique, choreography, costumes, hairstyle," Amma said tying the pink rubber band.

"But the glasses will disturb me," Meera said making a twirl.

"Appa got it fixed," Amma said, gently putting the thin elastic headband which was almost of the same color of Meera's hair.

"This would keep the glasses during movement and would not slide while you twirl and swirl."

* * * * *

SHOULD I?

"Are we ready?" Miss Sangeeta was checking the last touch ups for each participant.

"Yes ma'am," they all chorused.

All the little ballerinas dressed in pink tutu skirts and pink headband made the perfect batch.

"Pointed toes"

"Straight arms"

"Shoulders widen"

"Chin up"

"And no looking down," Miss Sangeeta gave the last-minute instructions.

Meera was still not sure about her glasses. She held the glasses in her hand.

Soon they all heard the claps for the previous performance, and it was their turn to go on stage.

"All the best children remember the stage is yours," Miss Sangeeta was excited as she patted each one of the group members.

The curtain was still down while the group took their place.

"Here, silly," Nitya chucked as she saw Meera standing in the wrong place.

Miss Sangeeta had put marks for each group member.

Meera squinted her eyes and saw the white chalk cross mark. She shifted and safely placed herself right.

She squinted more; she could see more marks.

"Children, remember to always place yourself on the line marks when you move forward and backward. This would help maintain the synchronisation." Miss Sangeeta was marking the cross-check marks all over the stage.

But to Meera, it looked all hazy.

All of a sudden, Meera again started to feel restless. Her ears buzzed. The tutu skirt made her stomach cramp and the hair bun made her head heavy.

"What shall I do with the glasses??"

"Remove them. You can see fine," the heart argued.

"But you will miss the marks," the mind corrected.

Before she could grasp her inside conversations and make a choice, it was Miss Sangeeta standing right in front of her.

"What is your plan for your glasses during the show?" Miss Sangeeta opened the subject.

"Would it disturb the unified group's look," Meera asked shyly.

"Why would it?"

"What's more important is that you should be comfortable and confident about it. Anyway, wouldn't it be better than a falling ballerina," Miss Sangeeta made it that simple with a smile.

The curtain raised.

The music began.

Meera put on her glasses.

She pulled in the muscle in her tummy,

tightened her leg muscles,

raised her toes to the tip,

widened her shoulders,

opened her arms,

and twirled like the world's finest ballerina.

THE PINK ELEPHANTS OF JAISALMER

Salini Vineeth

Jaisalmer is beige. They will tell you it's golden. But, believe me, it's beige. If you mix yellow ochre and burnt sienna, you will get the colour of Jaisalmer. How do I know it? I have learned painting while I was in school. But I didn't pursue it. Why did I stop? I can't remember.

But wait, you are not asking me about beige, right? You are asking me why Jaisalmer is beige. Why are we even talking about Jaisalmer? It's all a bit hazy in here.

Anyway, I know Jaisalmer is beige because I was there. Was it yesterday or two weeks back? Or am I still there - in Jaisalmer? Where am I? I can't quite say. Maybe if I stand up and peep out through that window, I will be able to tell you! But it seems difficult to move.

Someone's sitting on my neck. You know, the way kids sit, with their legs dangling from your shoulders? Do you have kids? I don't think I have kids. But I remember seeing those stick-thin legs, hanging from somewhere, with those glittery pink shoes swinging in a soothing rhythm. One loose end of the shoelace was dangling from the left leg. Where have I seen those legs?

The legs were swinging to some song. Yes, there was some song for sure. I can hear it playing in the back of my head.

"It's a radio, don't try to bluff me. I might be a hundred years old, but I have seen a radio," a sound hissed just after a song finished.

"Uncle-ji, this is a wireless speaker, not radio. You connect it to the phone. Yes, without wire, that's why it's called wireless," a familiar voice is ringing in my ears. Then a new song starts, the legs start swinging again.

"*Kachoris*! Hot, hot *Kachoris* of Pokhran," a holler cuts through the song.

Yes! I have been to Pokhran. I still remember the taste of those *Kachoris*. It was the last thing I ate. I am pretty sure about that. I ate *kachoris* in Pokhran. The Bluetooth speaker was singing in the background, and stick-thin legs with pink, glittery shoes were dangling in front of me. I remember the oscillation.

I think I was on a train. But, where did I get in from? Where was I going? My head starts spinning again.

Have you ever been to Pokhran? It's a funny place, you know.

"Po-Khraaaa-N," Try it with me.

"Po-Khraaaa-N," doesn't it sound like KABOOM? Like a nuclear bomb blasting. I see Buddha smiling. Wait a minute; it isn't a smile. It's a sneer. Do you know the difference?

"Po-Khraaaa-N," it's funny when you say it out, syllable by syllable. But why do I keep saying it? Why can't I stop saying Pokhran?

My head weighs like a ton. I wish I could just detach it and keep it away. Have you ever thought about that? Removing your head like a helmet? It would be really helpful when you try to sleep on a bus. What if people have detachable heads? What if they misplace it in some public place, for example, on a train? A train like the one I took from Delhi to Jaisalmer.

Delhi, Yes, it was Delhi. Now I remember! I took a train from Delhi to Jaisalmer. That's why I had passed through Pokhran.

"Po-Khraaaa-N," I keep saying it, and I giggle. My giggle is turning into a laugh. I am laughing aloud. I don't know how to stop it. My mouth is parched. My lungs might collapse. Still, I can't stop laughing.

Ok, I know what you are thinking. I think I concur. There's something wrong with me. I am not making any sense, do I?

I feel cluttered. It feels like I have a deluge in my brain. Everything is mixed up into a pulp, and it's seeping out through my nose and mouth. I try to keep my head steady with my hands, but I cannot move my hands. What the hell? Someone has tied me up - in a chair, in Jaisalmer! In the beige city, which they call golden.

Ok, my point is, someone has tied me up – hands and legs, both. I can't stop laughing. My heart might burst, and I might die. But before I do, I should try and remember who had tied me up.

Pay attention. You might be the last person I will ever talk to.

Who tied me up? Is it that turban-man on the train?

"Music travelling from your phone to this thing? Don't try to fool me," he laughed, showing off his pan-stained, wafer-thin teeth. The old fellow thought my Bluetooth speaker was a radio!

No, no. It can't be the turban-man. He is too stupid to do it. I had said goodbye to him at the Jaisalmer station. But was it today? Or was it a week back? How long have I been tied up in this pigeon hole? But, I ate those *kachoris* in Pokhran today morning so it can't be long.

"Po-Khraa-N, Ha, Ha," I know. I need to stop this evil laugh and get out of this room. Have you ever had a terror-struck laugh? That's what I am doing now! In between the outbursts of laughter, I am yelling and howling. It seems that no one is around.

I need to get out of this place. But, how? I look around, and I see my backpack leaning against the filthy wall. My phone and Bluetooth speaker are on a small teapoy next to it. I need to reach my phone, but I just can't move! Do you want to know something interesting? There is a hole in the opposite wall, and I can see the silhouette of the Jaisalmer fort.

It's a dingy room with a view! Oh, did I say it already? I don't remember.

Jaisalmer Fort. Yes! Someone had snatched my backpack and shoved it into a dirty autorickshaw - right in front of the Jaisalmer Fort. He pushed me into the auto and took a seat next to me. It's not the regular lemon-yellow and green rickshaws you find on Delhi roads. It was a beige autorickshaw. I told you everything in Jaisalmer is beige, even the rickshaws. It jerked, coughed, and jumped up like a demon getting ready to swallow me. There was a huge cloud of beige dust as the rickshaw finally took off.

By the way, did you know Dipika married Kapil on 23rd November 2013? Who are Dipika and Kapil? I have no idea. Maybe I am Dipika. My brain seems to be in a soup. Am I married to this Kapil? I have no idea. I am not even able to remember my name.

"If your husband were alive, would he allow such nonsense? Marry the girl off. She is thirty-two. She can become this solo traveller or whatever if her husband permits," I remember someone croaking. I remember Amma standing next to me, head hanging low.

I am trying hard to remember Amma's face. But only that gruff voice rings in my head. I am sure that I am not Dipika and definitely not married to Kapil.

I am sorry, I know, I need to focus. I may not have much time.

My legs are hurting under the tight knot. I need to try and remember the fellow who pushed me into that auto. I am trying my best but, my brain has started a police line-up—the first one is the face of that man who kept pinching my inner thigh in the back seat of a crowded K.S.R.T.C. bus. I was just eight years old. I thought I had forgotten that ugly face. Then it's the jeep driver who groped my breasts when I was in high school, the bus conductor who rubbed against me in the local bus and so many more hands those scratched every inch of my body in the last thirty-two years.

You might want to stand a little apart. I think I am going to puke.

"She should have kicked and screamed!" "Maybe it was consensual turned bad." "What better could happen for a girl who roams around alone?" "She should have been more careful." "Solo traveller, what nonsense is that?" "Doesn't she know India isn't safe for women? Hasn't she learned even after so many incidents?" I hear voices. They are echoing within the walls of this tiny room. I have heard all of them before, at different times. The sounds are clashing with each other as if played through multiple speakers.

Could you please muffle those voices? Could you please tell them to mind their own fucking business?

But, wait. Are you thinking the same about me? Do you think I am an irresponsible woman? Do you think it's my mistake to be trapped like this?

No, no, no. Please, don't go away, I didn't mean to accuse you. You are my last hope. Before he comes back, I need to tell you how that person looks. Maybe he is out to get his friends. I am sure they are going to harm me. They will rape me and burn me alive or strangle me.

I struggle in the chair, but the knots are just getting tighter. My head is spinning, and my throat is parched. I might die of thirst before they attack me. That would be a relief, don't you think? For you and me, I would rather die of thirst than being ripped apart. Do you remember that night in Delhi? The bus, the blunt metal object, ripping of the intestine. It's playing in front of me – beat by beat, like a movie.

My brain is getting larger every second. I am yelling at the top of my voice. But nobody is responding. Am I inside a well or something? All I can hear is the echo of my voice. But I won't go down without setting a trap for them. I need to find something, some clue about the man who dragged me here. I don't want that rascal escape after he has ripped me apart.

Multi-lingual – I remember that visiting card. A red piece of paper with cyan letters popping out of it. Red and cyan - those colours, they go really well with each other.

"You are good at mixing colours," my painting teacher had once said. I remember his face and his bold strokes. Now I remember why I didn't finish my painting class. My teacher was arrested; they said he was a liberal, an anti-national. He was arrested and was never seen again. Poof! He was gone just like that. What you call it? Vanished into thin air, Right? Or if you have read 1984, he was just vaporized.

So, what was I saying? I wish I could be more coherent. But you know, I cannot control the speed and direction of my thoughts. They are running around, like kids in a primary school during the recess.

Please, remind me what was I saying? No, not my painting teacher. Before that.

Yes, the visiting card. It was a small square piece of paper with a few words printed on it. But I only remember the word multi-lingual. What else was written on that card? It's all ripped up like the pieces of a jigsaw puzzle.

Have you ever played a jigsaw puzzle in your childhood? I had plenty of them. I was good at solving them. This might be the most important jigsaw I ever solve in my life. I need to focus and remember it. I can almost see those cyan letters, but all those pieces are floating around me.

'Cling!' Someone has dropped a glass in the next room! I think I don't have much time. The clang of the metal reminds me of something. His voice. It was a high-pitched voice like coins rattling inside an empty can.

"*Maidam*," that's what he had called me. I remember that peculiar syllable in the middle of it. He had called me *Maidam*. Not once, several times. I am sure he is the one who had pushed me into that rickshaw in front of the Jaisalmer Fort.

Multi-lingual, first-class tourist guide, yes, that's what was written on the visiting card. Do you know any first-class, multi-lingual tourist guide in Jaisalmer? You will have to find out. Or, remember this phrase and pass it to the police when I am dead.

I am pretty sure they will not leave me alive. It's a botheration, right? I will go to the court, I will testify against them, I will become yet another -maybe the 100th, I reckon - icon of women safety. If they don't finish me now, they will have to go through the trouble of finishing me later – throwing acid on my face or burning me alive or hitting me with a truck! It's a pain for everyone, right?

Ok, I know I am talking all over the place. But I am horrified. Have you ever felt really horrified? Horrified to the extent that you don't know if you are alive or dead? Don't worry, don't bother to answer now. There is no time.

Get a pen and write this down - *multi-lingual, first-class tourist guide*, printed on a red visiting card in cyan letters.

Will they be able to find the culprit by just this one clue? I doubt. They are not Sherlock Holmes! Do you want to know something? I am a Sherlock fan. I have read the entire works.

Shall I tell you a secret? I like Watson more. Sherlock is a bossy know-it-all. But Watson is a real friend. I wish I had a Watson – a friend who never leaves my side, a man who hugs me without brushing my buttocks or pushing my breasts. I have met no man like Watson. Hence, I am not married.

Is it why they call me a failure in my family circles?

Why can't I stop crying now? I feel like some funny pixie is jumping up and down in my brain, running through its coils, poking, and tickling. Look at me, sitting tied to a chair in a stink-hole in the golden city of Jaisalmer, which is not even golden.

I know I have to hurry up. Time is running out. I need to think and remember his name. But wait a minute. How will they find my body? Charred and hidden inside the bushes near the *Khaba* fort? Or on the railway tracks on the outskirts of Jaisalmer? My brain is racing ahead of me.

I need water. Now! I feel like I can drink up an entire ocean.

Ocean, yes, he had told me something about the ocean. I am trying to shoo away my brain pixie and remember what the first-class, multi-lingual tour guide had told me in his rattling voice.

"*Maidam*, I haven't seen the beach. I have lived in Jaisalmer my whole life. I want to see the beach. That's my dream."

Has he tied me up for money? I wish it were the case. My legs are lifting from the floor, and I am floating around in the scanty room. I am afraid I would hit the fan or the walls. How do I stop it? Before I pass out, I need to tell you a few things about this multi-lingual, first-class tourist guide. I remembered them just now.

He is tall. Very tall. He might be over six feet. While we visited the Jain temples inside the Jaisalmer Fort, I had to crane my neck to look at his face. Tourist guides shouldn't be that tall. They should be around five-five or less so that it's comfortable for short people to follow what they are saying.

Oh, no, I am floating towards one of the walls. I hit the wall and hurt my head. I am bouncing back and forth between the walls of this scanty room. I think I am going to pass out soon.

What was I saying? Yes, this guy is very tall. Then his teeth – they are pearl white, unlike the tobacco-stained tooth of men here. His hair is thin and kind of a copper colour. The way it stays on the top of his head reminds me of grass sticking out of a haystack. His ears are pierced, and he is wearing studs with red stones. Don't forget when the police ask you. I think you have more than enough clues to recognize him. I will list it again – first-class, multi-lingual tourist guide, very tall, no tobacco stain on his teeth, haystack head, and pierced ears with red-stone stud.

Are you taking note of all these? Hurry up; I think my time's up.

I hear the clanking of the tin door. I can hear his steps. I suddenly fall from the air with a thud. My tongue sticks to the roof of my mouth. I wriggle on the chair, but the knots keep cutting into my skin.

The door opens, and there he is. He isn't alone. There is another fellow behind him- a short fellow, wearing a beige sweater. Didn't I tell you everything is beige in Jaisalmer?

Should I laugh or cry? My heart is flapping loud against my chest like a bird trapped inside a carton box. So, this is it. They are walking towards me: the first-class tourist guide and the beige-sweater guy.

"*Maidam*," I shudder as he calls me. See, I told you there is a peculiar syllable in the middle of Madam. His studs are glittering in the evening sun seeping through the small hole in the wall. A sour liquid is rising in my throat.

Are you still there? Are you listening?

"*Maidam*, who are you talking to? Have this." He is shoving a small bowl in my face. It has some brown powder. What is it? Is it roofies? Have you heard of roofies – the date-rape drug?

"Is it roofies?" I yell at him as he prepares to untie me. Surprisingly, I am not terrified anymore. I am feeling stronger than ever. The moment he unties me, I will grab that iron rod near the wall and split his head into two. I am not going down without a fight. That's what people anyway want, right? "Why didn't she kick and scream?" They ask.

"Maidam, I don't know what you mean. This is the bhungra powder, please have it," I hear his rattling voice again.

What's *bhungra*? Maybe it's a local version of roofies. He is telling me 'please' while trying to force-feed me the date-rape drug? How presumptuous! He is shoving the bowl again into my face. My mouth is shut tight. He seems to be a little perplexed. He steps back.

"*Bhang mange bhungra, ganja mange ghee, daru mange juta,*" the beige-sweater is singing a folk song and laughing at me. How presumptuous of him too!

"Stop your bloody song," I start shrieking.

"*Maidam,* it's not a song. It's a proverb. *bhungra* – the roasted gram – will help you sober up. You need to eat it," he opens my mouth by force and feeds me some of that nutty powder.

"Sober up? What the hell you mean?" I am struggling to breathe as I gulp down something that tastes like peanuts. I am chocking on the fine powder. I might faint now. He unties my legs, and I kick hard in his shin. He yelps and crawls towards the wall.

"She is still under... let's come back after sometime, *bhungra* will take time to start working," the beige sweater is telling the top-class guide.

"Under what?" I violently shake my body and scream at them. The beige-sweater is standing a bit far and grinning. I wish if he had come nearer. He will also see the moon and stars when I kick him.

"*Maidam*, don't you remember anything? Do you remember me? Panchu - Your tour guide?" Yes! His name is Panchu. Don't forget this. His name is Panchu. He is the one who showed me around Jaisalmer Fort and then pushed me into a beige rickshaw.

"You scoundrel, why have you abducted me? Do you want money?" Panchu looks up at me. He is crouching on the floor. My kick is doing its job. I wouldn't go down without a fight, I promise. I will not beg for mercy.

"Oh my God, she doesn't remember a thing," the beige-sweater is clutching his stomach and laughing. His howling is ringing in my ears like the siren of death. This is how they show it in the movies. The villains love to taunt their prey.

Panchu seems worried. He asks the beige-sweater to shut up. Then he goes out like wind while the beige-sweater stands guard. I feel really dizzy now. I am sweating and panting. I need to drink some water. My eyes are fading. But I cannot go down without a fight. I wouldn't make it easy for them. I will not faint.

"*Maidam*," Panchu is back. He has a glass of water and my camera. My Nikon DSLR. What is he trying to do with it?

"Take it if you want, take everything, take the money, take the camera, my credit card," I hate myself for crying in front of them. I don't think I can hold on any longer.

"Maidam, please, don't cry. Look at these photos. I am going to come near, please don't kick me again," Panchu is begging me. I am so confused now.

He comes near and flicks through the photos on my Nikon– the turban-man in the train, the stick-thin legs with the pink and glitter shoes, *kachoris* broken in half-steaming hot, Panchu in front of the Jaisalmer Fort, the Jain temples, and the museum.

"*Maidam*, look at this photo, you will remember everything," Panchu flicks right and stops.

It's a photo of me standing in front of a shop with a metal board. "Government Approved Bang Shop," the name board says. I am holding a glass full of some green liquid. I am gleaming.

Panchu stops for a while and then flicks past – The images are getting a bit shaky. The beige auto, the poster in front of a haveli that says "Dipika weds Kapil, 23/11/2017", faces of Panchu and the beige-sweater sitting in front of the auto, Ajay's goat leather shop, and a flight of narrow steps.

"I don't believe this. You might have tricked me into drinking it. Why did you tie me up?" I ask Panchu. I am not able to believe my eyes.

"Maidam, I am sorry, I didn't know you were trying bhang for the first time. You got high and started creating ruckus in front of the Jaisalmer Fort. I didn't want the police to arrest you. I called Ram's auto. But you refused to get into it. So, I had to use some force. All the while, you kept clicking photos like crazy," Panchu stopped and gulped. He cautiously moves away from me.

"If you wanted to protect me, then why did you tie me up?" I ask again. Ram – the beige sweater –is laughing again.

"I am sorry, Maidam, you insisted it. You told you were flying up and would hit the ceiling fan. You were screaming. You calmed down only after I tied you to the chair," Panchu finished with a sigh and started to untie me. My eyes slowly closed with exhaustion.

* * * * *

"*Maidam*, I am really sorry for what happened I shouldn't have locked you up in the room and go in search of bhungra. I should've at least called my wife," Panchu is standing next to the window of the train. I had slept five hours straight. Thankfully I could make it to the Jaisalmer-Delhi express in time.

"No, Panchu, I should apologize. I thought you were going to harm me. I kicked you! Do you know what everyone says? They say I am crazy. I think they are right. I shouldn't have tried the bhang. Maybe, this solo travelling, I am not smart enough to do it." I absolutely have no idea why I am venting out to Panchu.

I wish the train starts soon so that Panchu will not have to console me.

"Maidam, while you were under bhang, you kept saying one thing; that you love this life and don't want to go back to your desk job. You told me that travelling is your thing. So, don't stop doing it,"

I swear I have no idea telling all that. Maybe Panchu is making it up.

The train has started moving. I am saying goodbye to Panchu. But there is one more thing I need to know.

"Panchu, are you really multi-lingual?" I holler at him.

"Oui, Madame. French and German," He shouts back. There is no funny syllable in the middle of madame. Panchu is smiling at me, showing off his pearl-white teeth and his glittery red stud.

I hope he will be able to see the ocean soon.

THE BRAIN SURGEON

Sudheendra Fadnis

It was 1950's when the practice of lobotomy (the practice of slicing off the portions of Prefrontal cortex to cure mental ailments especially epilepsy) was in full swing. Dr. Antonio was one of those neuroscientists who had the uncanny ability to peep into the neurological conditions of his patients with sharp logic and deep empathy. He had grown up reading the works of great philosophers, psychologists and thinkers of his time and used to day dream that he would contribute to the neuroscience someday to make this world a better place. The human brain has always remained an enigma to him. He would sometimes wonder at night, before going to sleep, how come this fatty organ hardly weighing 3 pounds could give rise to feelings, sensations, thoughts and creativity. Over the period of years, he almost developed an unrelenting obsession for the neuroscience subject.

Psychology studies the mind, but he wanted to study the brain. Psychiatry didn't allure him though. He had grown sick of the subject seeing some of his own kith and kin suffer from psychosis at a very young age. His interest was in decoding the secrets of the brain. His career plans were intact; he would study general medicine first to understand how the human body works. Because he knew that without understanding the body, he could not understand the brain. Everything was planned and went according to the plan. He was destiny's child in that way. He developed audacious ambitions once he completed residency from the John Hopkins Medical School. He would become one of the world's best neurosurgeons. He had it in him and he knew that. Apart from being a man of brains, he was also a man of dexterity. His hands were strong enough to get into a bout when provoked, repair those air coolers and other gadgets when required and also give a soothing touch to the patients who didn't need just treatment but love. Time passed by. He became a Neurosurgeon specializing in neuro-oncology (Brain Cancer).

But there was something very unusual about him. There were certain secrets about him which only he knew and kept it to himself. He knew that he was special, at the same time unusual. He had quirks which made him idiosyncratic. But he never let those quirks come in way of his career growth trajectory. He knew that he would be great at neuroscience one day. It was only a matter of time. He still could not forget the day of his convocation when he got the honorary badge from none other than Elkhonon Goldberg, the legendary neuroscientist who spent his entire lifetime studying the hemispherisation theory of the brain. And he got his surgery license too.

He has spent his college days dissecting frogs, the brains of monkeys and examining the cadavers of the forsaken bodies in the laboratories. It never appalled him. Rather, like Leonardo da Vinci, it excited him. During one of the days as usual, his phone rang and he answered. It was a call from his senior resident Mr. Oliver about a patient whose glial cell growth has gone out of bounds resulting in malignant tumours which can prove to be life-threatening if left un-operated. Mr. Oliver said in an authoritative tone: You must be there in the surgery.

The surgery day arrived sooner than later. It was Friday. He was ready. He woke up early in the morning. His conscience was pricking him for some unusual reason. He didn't know why. He had his breakfast as usual and headed straight to John Hopkins where the entire operation apparatus was set up. He headed straight to the ward the patient was laying on the bed. He went straight to him and said, "I am Antonio and I will be performing the surgery for you." He then grasped his hand. There was a sparkle on the patient's face. After the formalities, he personally assisted the patient in lying down on the bed.

The time has come and everybody was up for surgery. The patient was taken into the surgery room. Mr. Vijay, an Indian anaesthetist administered the optimal dose of anaesthesia so that the operation could be initiated. Antonio took the measurements of the size of the brain. He then looked at the FMRI scans of the patient's brain which clearly showed that the patient had developed tumours in the hippocampus because of which his memory was getting dwindled and distorted at the same time. It was time to drill the skull. Too much of rough handling can make the patient dead and too little can make the surgery complicated. He did the drilling of the skull as if Michelangelo would sculpt a David with every stroke.

He was panting heavily. Nervousness was just not his style. Was something ominous about the operation? He didn't know, but his soul stirred him deeply. He had the feeling of butterflies running in his stomach. He had an impeccable reputation of being a great neurosurgeon, loved by his colleagues, junior residents and the patients alike. But he was feeling a deep existential void at the time of the operation. It was a mixed bag of feelings for him. They did not deter him though from his unwavering focus. He went on and on as if every second could not be snatched away, even by God. His colleagues of the operation team, how much ever immersed they might be in the operation were agape at his monomaniacal focus, thus restraining themselves to compliment him on the operation floor. His instructions were curt and sometimes even blunt as he did not want to compromise at any cost about saving the patient's life which, when operating, mattered more than his own life. He was a paragon of excellence when it came to his dedication towards the duty.

Finally, he opened the brain, the most magnificent of all the creations in the universe. Wearing the hand gloves, and aided by robotic technology, he could access the hippocampus-a small structure deep inside the limbic system. It was unusually big because of the malignant tumours. Then, as he took his surgical knife to slice off those tumours with mechanical precision, something unusual happened. He could see the patient's life in 3d images. He could see how the patient had a loving family, and his mother fondling him when he was a child. The funny quarrels that he would have with his chubby sister, how luckily, he ended up on the bed with his teenage crush when he was 18, and as he grew his strained relationship with his wife and children who wouldn't care about him because of his illness. He was deluded with all these images. Dr. Antonio really had trouble distinguishing reality from the patient's life. Was he hallucinating? Was he cursed with those damned psychotic genes from kith and kin? Who knows? Luckily, his sanity was intact enough to make him realize that he was in charge of operation and he took few deep breaths and continued the operation to success. It took him full two hours to complete the operation with his team.

By the time he was out of the operation theatre, he was exhausted emotionally, spiritually and physically. What about the fate of the patient? Was the operation successful? Yes and No. The patient was both alive and dead. He was alive biologically speaking, but had become like a zombie left to the mercy of his unloving family. His family would treat him like a burden. He was like orphan with a family. His opinions would not be heard any more. Nobody would by sit his side to tell him what had happened during the day. No more were the heart to heart talks with his family at the prime of his life. His zest to life has evaporated with each insult that he had borne. He missed the man Dr. Antonio who had given him so much hope, only to see himself devastated by the cruel emotional neglect of his family. Dr. Antonio would enquire with the juniors of his, at times, as he was deeply concerned about the patient. It left his colleagues wonder why this was so.

Little did they know that there was a deeply hidden secret about him that could jeopardise his career forever, and proving to be a death knell to his ambitions and zeal to be an instrument of service to the world through his knowledge and dexterity. After several months of his operation, one night, Mr. Antonio made a note in his journal:

I don't know how I performed that surgery. It was as if I am in a state of deep flow, possessed by an unknown demon or by some supernatural force making me a puppet in its hands. It was clear that I was not hallucinating, for it would have totally rendered me dysfunctional making me a despicable disgrace to the society. Let us see for how long this saga shall go on. Adieu for now.

WRONG NUMBER

Swapnil Saurav

The long drives in heavy traffic and a whole hectic week drained Rahul as he dragged out his exhausted body from his car on a Friday night. The week had been the most stressful week of his entire career. It was in this same week his company bagged four contracts which had never happened before, and to meet up with the deadlines, they had to up their dedications, time spent at work, and all.

He unlocked the door and turned the knob. Slamming it behind him with a little frustration, he proceeded to slump in his most loved armchair and tossed his briefcase on the table. It was a dark and quiet Friday night. For some people, Friday nights are a chance to go out and have fun. It was a nice way to spend the remaining energy that was left after their work week. But not so for Rahul. Rahul was already all out of his energy. He really needed some time to sit comfortably in his armchair, absorb the silence around him and enjoy the feeling of relaxation. This single moment of peace was worth all the work he did this week. Minutes after he had settled, he felt his focus diminish.

Suddenly, the Zen-like aura of peace was pierced by an unexpected noise. It was his phone. He woke with a start despite the fact that he had no memory of dozing off. He floated into consciousness. And after that, he blacked out again. The blare of the phone immediately jolted him back to the outside world. He couldn't keep focus; his eyes were heavy.

Rahul immediately stood up and cast a surprised eye at his watch, which showed that the time was close to half past eleven. He wasn't used to receiving phone calls at this time of night. He wondered who it could be. His thoughts started jumping around in his mind trying to connect the dots and figure out who it might be before checking it out. He couldn't remember if he was expecting any calls. It was likely just a wrong number. It happens often and it could happen to anyone, so it wasn't anything strange.

"Hello, it is Rahul," his voice was as heavy as an elephant's. He rubbed his eyes with the palm of his other hand and waited to hear the voice of the person on the line.

"This is KIMS Hospital Kondapur. Your friend Lokesh just met with an accident and he'd want you here. He needs a major operation."

Rahul steered into reality. Lokesh? Accident? How's that possible?

"Accident? What are you talking about? See, I had a rough week, very rough in fact. So, I'd want no one to play pranks on me. Please." Rahul couldn't think of anything to say other than that.

"Your friend Lokesh got in an accident. He wants you here at the KIMS hospital."

And the line went dead. Rahul couldn't believe his ears. Everybody knows these things happen, but you never suspect it will ever happen to you. As if time completely stood still, Rahul couldn't move at first, but he soon started rushing to the hospital.

Rahul looked upwards, his mouth tightened however marginally open and free. His eyes were fixed as though he was taking a look at something. Before he could consider anything better, he snatched the vehicle key on the table and dashed out, not minding his weariness or his urge to sleep. His best friend was in danger and he had to get to him fast. On the way, his mind was filled with awful images and he was very worried for his friend. He was praying for his friend, hoping everything would end well. He remembered that a car accident caused this problem in the first place, so he slowed down a bit.

Rahul finally reached the hospital, standing still for a moment and tried to gather up courage to go inside. The automatic door opened, and he stepped inside slowly. The hospital lobby looked very much like the rest of the emergency clinic. The floor was slate dim and the walls dove. The roof was produced using polystyrene squares. The light was unreasonably bright for his eyes after the obscuring anguish outside, he thought that it was grating, enough maybe to bring back one of his headaches. There were commercial prints on the wall, elegant in a dull sort of way. Over each door he passed was a substantial plastic sign, dim with white lettering - no extravagant text styles, simply striking and all-caps. He approached the nurses in the hall and explained his situation to them. They told him to be patient and that everything will be fine. One nurse showed him the direction to the emergency ward. Rather than straight walls, the lobby had a bend, vanishing from sight in a hundred metres or somewhere in the vicinity. At regular intervals he passed an alternate arrangement of doors with a hand sanitizer: to oncology, to geriatrics, to maternity. He avoided them all setting out towards accident and emergency, since that was the place Lokesh was. Accident and emergency, wide passage with programmed sliding glass doors, ambulances parked outside, paramedics wheeling in patients on wheelchairs, one was a child in a neck support, another child was shouting in the passageways, and the doctor came running.

Rahul talked with the nurse at the reception and was told his friend was undergoing surgery. He paid the bill in advance. He didn't even ask how much it costs, because money means nothing compared to health and especially life. It is interesting how people never think about their health until an accident happens or until it is too late. He never liked hospitals because they reminded him of being sick. Everything was white and smelled like medicine. It made him kind of anxious. Hospitals are a place where people go when they have health problems or something bad happens and just the fact that he was standing inside one was stressful for him. He felt his knees give in. He was walking in circles in the waiting room, sweating nervously.

After some time, Rahul sat on an empty chair. Sitting in the waiting room for a considerable length of time, he felt like he would die of anxiety the next minute. The clattering of the keys produced by the nurse, and the consistent exhausting ads from the TV was making him crazy. He needed to realise what was happening with his friend right at that point, not ten minutes, two hours or after ten years; he needed to know before his brain shut down. As he gazed at the clear white wall before him and attempted to think, he felt the pressure and tension develop in him as he gazed vacantly, his mind brimming with void. Before the frenzy could decimate him, he figured out how to make up for the lost time with inconspicuous breathing exercises to enable him to relax. Similarly, as he recovered his unfaltering heartbeat by taking in through the nose and out through the mouth, he could hear the constant tap of a heel against the floor and his heartbeat rate shot up by and by, after acknowledging what was nearing. Lokesh was in the theatre. Would he survive? What are his chances? He wished someone could give an answer to that.

After another hour, he saw some surgeons in blue coats coming out of the theatre. He rushed down to meet one of them.

"How's he? How's Lokesh? Will he be fine?" He rattled off the questions without minding if the beautiful lady doctor he was talking to, got his message.

"He will be fine. Will you see me in my office? Just follow closely."

"Yes."

What did she want to tell him? His heart raced again. Doctors cannot be trusted, he thought. Rahul entered the office following the doctor. The doctor went ahead to her burgundy seat and dropped her weight on it.

"Please have your seat, Mr..." the doctor said.

"Rahul Goel," completed Rahul, sitting on the chair and looking confusingly at the doctor.

Doctor then explained the situation and the medication that needed to be given to Lokesh. Rahul patiently took all the notes in his mobile phone. Doctor said, "I need to go out to see other patients. Please wait here, the nurse will inform you when you can meet your friend," and she walked out.

The office was so neat that you could sleep on the bare floor. But sleep was not on Rahul's mind. He looked at the clock and it was already 2 a.m. A nurse walked in. She informed Rahul that Lokesh is out of danger and led him to the room where his friend Lokesh was in bed. He was covered in bandages. Rahul looked at him with eyes full of tears and his vision was blurry. He couldn't even recognize Lokesh's face from all those tears. When his vision cleared out, he was shocked. This wasn't his Lokesh! They were both very confused. It appeared that it really was the wrong number all along!

Nurses arrived and explained the whole situation. They kept apologising but said it was a very stressful situation and mistakes can happen by anyone. The hospital made a mistake and dialled the wrong number; in the hurry they entered one digit wrong. They accidentally reached him, Rahul Goel, while they intended to reach Rahul Bajaj, this Lokesh's friend. And destiny wasn't over yet. It turned out that there are 2 people named Rahul who both have a friend called Lokesh! A different Rahul and a different Lokesh! It was a 1 in a million chance, but it happened. Rahul's worrying was over. But he still had one last job to do.

He called Rahul Bajaj to bring an end to this misunderstanding. He waited patiently and the two Rahuls met at last. Bajaj thanked Goel for his compassion and help and said that he was lucky that the hospital contacted such a good man, even though by an accident. It could have been someone who wasn't as good. He gave him money to pay back the operation charges. This was a very emotionally and physically draining night for Rahul. He definitely wasn't expecting this would happen when he woke up this morning.

What an end after such a busy week! But Rahul was not angry or sad. Even though he was tired, he was pleased with the good deed he did this night. He went home with a smile on his face, and he sat back on his armchair. He couldn't stop smiling until he fell asleep later that night, because Rahul knows that we can never know what will happen to us, but it is important to be a good and kind person, no matter what happens. Of course, helping a friend is a very good feeling, but we must not remember that it is important to help strangers, too. After all, we never know that strangers may become our friends someday.

WAITING ROOM

Krishna Ahir

The gurney clattered past Zumi, her last chance leaving with the man on it.

"You don't understand!" She cried, trying to reach past the nurse blocking her. "I have to talk to him!"

"He'll be out of surgery in a few hours, ma'am. You'll have to wait till then," the nurse said with an irritating calm. "There's a waiting room across the hall for family members. You'll be comfortable there."

At the end of the hall, the doors swung shut behind the leaving gurney. Zumi stood blankly, watching where it had gone. Satisfied, that she was no longer a threat, the nurse nodded, striding back behind the walls of her station.

Zumi turned towards the waiting room, feeling out of place as a 35-year-old in a red cocktail dress, her elaborate updo wilted. The dozens of eyes watching her all hastily flicked away to magazines, shoes, anything to pretend her little display hadn't been the most fascinating thing to happen to them in hours. It must be a busy day at the hospital, as few of the chairs were vacant. One of the few empty seats was next to a man smirking as he read the newspaper. At least he wasn't one of the many still gaping at her. Good enough, Zumi decided, and headed for the seat, wilfully blind to the many eyes following her.

As she sat, the newspaper crinkled next to her. "Did you get the drama out of your system? Or do I need to move seats before you start sobbing on my shoulder?"

Zumi gaped at the man. Still, he kept his gaze fixed on his newspaper, his eyes steadily flicking across the words. "Of all the rude, inconsiderate—"

He folded the newspaper. "Changing seats it is, then."

"Sit," Zumi snapped. "Don't you dare move because of me."

One of his eyebrows rose intrigued by the challenge. He said nothing, simply flicked his newspaper back open and resumed reading.

Zumi drummed her fingers on the lacquered wooden arm of her waiting room chair. There were hours to go, and not even a phone or a purse with which to distract herself. On the table next to her were a pile of magazines. She picked the first one up. Parenting. Grimacing, she exchanged it for the next. The man glanced at her. Baby Talk. Pantomiming retching, she let all her hopes fall to the third and final magazine. Snowboarding. Good enough. Zumi picked it up, leafing through its pages. The newspaper crinkled as the man raised it higher. According to the magazine, Nitro boards were apparently a steal. And of course Deadbolt snowboard boots were overrated, but always reliable. At least there were a few pictures of mountains.

When she flipped the magazine upside down, the man could no longer restrain himself. "What an original way to see a story from a new angle."

Zumi glared at him. "As if you'd know, reading the same section of Finance for the third time."

"Health, actually," he said, folding the paper. "And it was only the second. Do you board?"

"More than I Parent," she said, gesturing to the discarded magazines. A smile quirked at his lips, "do you Health?"

He gestured to himself; trim in buttoned shirt, tie, and slacks. "I am the epitome of healthiness."

"Lankiness," she muttered.

"Excuse me?"

"You heard me."

A silence stretched. Zumi fiddled with the cover of Snowboarding, unsure whether to open it again. The idea wasn't very tempting.

"I'm Zahi."

Zumi turned, surprised by the gesture. "Zumi."

He cleared his throat. "Do I want to know what was happening, before?"

"You made it abundantly clear that you don't," she snapped, turning away once more.

Zahi waited a moment before trying again. "Could you say it without getting emotional?"

An irritated huff burst from her. "There's nothing emotional about it! It was a blind date. He still has my necklace. The end."

"A blind date?" Zahi asked. Zumi nodded. "So you're stuck waiting here for…?"

"A stranger, that's right."

Zahi slipped the folded newspaper into his briefcase. "And how on earth did this stranger get your necklace?"

"It broke!" Zumi tossed her hands into the air. "I don't have any pockets, so he kept it for me."

Zahi made a face, leaning forward onto his thighs. "That's immensely impractical. What would you have done if he'd been a bore? You can't even call a cab to go home."

"I have cash on me. I'm not an idiot."

"If you don't have pockets, how in the world -" He cut off as Zumi started to reply, raising his hand to stop her. "Don't tell me. I'd rather keep my innocence."

Zumi snorted. "So what are you in here for, fish?"

A smirk toyed with his lips. "You'd never guess."

With a sigh, Zumi leaned back in her chair. "Correct again. In a hospital, every guess is morbid."

"Killjoy. I'm a doctor."

Disbelief covered Zumi's face. "Out here? With all us peasants?"

Zahi shrugged. "I just need a lab report and I can head home. Never figured it would take this long to process."

"Don't doctors have break rooms? Where they serve caviar and admire the snap of a fresh latex glove?"

His face turned sour. "And where they're throwing the third baby shower this month."

"Ah." Zumi paused, not sure how to proceed delicately. "And you're not...?"

"Enraptured by squalling lumps of flesh? No."

"Married"

He snorted. "Also no." He glanced at Zumi, still looking lovely in her dress, despite being of his own age. "What's your excuse? I thought everyone had settled or given up."

She looked down at her hands laced in her lap, wishing she had something better than a magazine to fiddle with. "Maybe they're the smart ones."

Zahi felt an uncomfortable bout of emotions occurring and tried to backpedal. "You just went on a blind date. That's... brave?"

Zumi made a face at him. "Let me know how brave you feel when your blind date is so desperate to get away from you that he poisons himself."

Zahi choked. "I'm sorry?"

She sighed. "The *enrapturing* fellow started off the evening proudly listing all his allergies for the benefit of myself and the wait staff. Then, the *moment* he stopped talking about himself long enough for me to get a proper introduction in, he found it so ridiculous that I'd be a software designer that he asked for the joke's punch line!"

Zahi paused. "At which point he poisoned himself to supply one for you?"

With a groan, Zumi flopped back in her chair. "At which point I got so angry that I threw my napkin at him. I proceeded to crack *hilarious* software designer jokes until he thought his only way out was cyanide – or in his case, a strawberry. After I *saw* him reach into the appetizer in the *middle* of the table, he very loudly announced what an accident it had been and that his face was swelling so badly he'd have to go home. Only, by then, it wasn't just his face. His throat was swelling, too, and he couldn't finish his sentence around his bloated tongue. The restaurant had to call the paramedics."

Zahi tried to keep a straight face – for about two seconds. Hand covering his mouth, he collapsed into laughter.

"Laugh it up at the harpy," Zumi glared.

"I'm glad he has your necklace," Zahi chuckled, wiping tears of mirth from his eyes. "Fitting payback."

Zumi tossed the snowboarding magazine back onto the end table. "He was awful, anyway. I'll never understand what my friends saw in him."

Zahi shrugged. "Our age and single, is my guess. That's all my last date and I had in common."

"Oh ho! The good doctor mingles with the rest of the world?"

He shrugged again, a hint of a smile playing with his lips. "I think she wished she had a strawberry allergy."

Zumi laughed. It had been awhile since she'd laughed like that, and certainly not with a stranger. Zahi watched her, pleased by her enjoyment. The little hopeful seed that she'd buried in her heart so long ago sprouted a tiny green shoot.

"Dr. Baig?"

The voice of the nurse shocked Zumi out of her moment. The same nurse from before stood next to Zahi, a file in her outstretched hand.

"Sorry, it took me so long to find you," the nurse continued. "I thought you'd be at Kelsey's party with the rest of the staff. Here's the blood work you wanted."

Zahi took the file, flipping through it with a perfunctory glance. "Perfect. Thank you."

He stood, grabbing his briefcase. And before Zumi even had a chance to say goodbye... he was gone.

She doused the green sprout with gasoline, relishing in its blackening corpse. She was fine living alone, she told herself for the thousandth time. She had a fulfilling job, nieces and nephews that she loved, and maybe she'd get a second dog. To keep her other dog from being lonely, of course.

Angrily, she opened her snowboarding magazine. Zumi tried to read, but the words in front of her blurred together in an angry haze. Men were the worst. Even rude, obnoxious-

A silver chain dropped into her lap, the raptor charm dangling from it all-too-familiar.

"My necklace!" Zumi cried, looking up. All words stopped at the sight. Zahi stood over her, grinning that stupid smug grin. "How did you...?"

"Went back there and asked. There has to be some benefit in being a doctor." His eyes glittered with mischief. "Want to get out of here? I know a place with terrific strawberries."

ISHARA

Shakeeb Ahmad

Poltu ek alag qism ka bachcha hai. Umra 10 saal aur apne maa ke saath akela rehta hai. Chauthe maalay pe zyadatar Poltu balcony mein baithke pinjday mein band kabutar ko dekhta rehta aur na jane unki hi bhasha mein kuch na kuch bolta rehta hai.

Poltu theek se bol nahi pata lekin parindon ki awaaz bakhoobi nikaal leta hai. Poltu ko insaan samajh nahi aate lekin apni maa se uski mohabbat ek alag hi tarah ki hoti hai. Poltu school bhi nahi jata. uska social interaction na hone ki wajah se school waalay home schooling ka option de dete hain.

Jaya usko ghar pe hi leke rehti hai aur ek tarah ki home schooling set up mein usko rakhti hai. .Jaya ki divorce ka process bhi chal raha hai aur saath ke saath woh ek private firm mein accountant bhi hai. Sham tak aate aate daer ho jaati hai toh woh ghar ka saara kaam jaise Poltu ke liye khana aur baaqi saari cheezen kar ke jaati hai.

Poltu balcony se Jaya ko bye karta hai aur phir uske aane tak balcony mein hi baitha rehta hai. Dher saaray parinday uske dost hain jo uski balcony mein baithe rehte hain aur woh unse baat karta rehta hai. Pata nahi kya baat lekin khush rehta hai uska saara waqt unke saath guzarta hai.

Poltu ki balcony aisi hoti hai jahan se usko saamne ka park aur garden saaf saaf dikhte jahan woh logon ko exercise karte dekhta hai kabhi couples ko pyar mohabbat karte toh kabhi apni hi umra ke bachchon ko cricket yaa badminton khelte dekhta hai. woh balcony aur woh parinday aur Jaya bass itni hi duniya uski hoti hai.

Ek din Poltu ek Giddh ko apni balcony se dekhta hai jo uske apartment ke saamne se taezi se udd ke nikal jata hai. Poltu pehli baar kisi parinday ko dekh ke sahem jata hai. Phir thodi der baad woh Giddh wapas apni badisi choonch mein ek kabutar ko leke aata hua ekdum uski balcony ke paas se guzarta hai.

Poltu darr ke maaray ghar ke ander aa jata hai aur apne kabutaron pe ek motisi chaader daal deta hai. .Jaya ko woh batane ki koshish karta hain lekin Jaya kisi aur uljhan mein rehti hai aur uski baat ko samajh nahi paati.

Phir kuch din baad Poltu usi Giddh ko Watchman ke sarr pe udte dekhta hai aur woh sahem jata hai. jaldi se woh darwaza khol ke neechay utartaa hai aur lift se utar ke watchman ko bulata hai isharay se watchman aata hai aur usko dekh bolta hai jao upar, mummy shaam ko aaegi.

Poltu apni garden pakad ke phir uski garden dabaa ke kuchh samjhana chahata hai maano woh keh rahaa ho tumhari jaan khatre mein hai lekin watchman ko Jaya bolke rakhti hai ke Poltu ka ilaaj chal raha hai isko bahar mat jane dena. Watchman Poltu ko flat tak chhorr ke darwaza bahar se band karke Jaya ko call karke batata hai Jaya usko thank you bolti hai.

Phir agle hi din watchman ki laash garden mein milti hai aur uski gardan ka gosht poora bahar niklaa hota hai maano jaise kisi ne nochliya ho. Log pareshan hotay hain police logon se sawaal jawab karti hai aur watchman ki lash ko wahan se le jaati hai. Jaya Poltu se poochti hai aisa kya hua tha kyu gaye the neechay watchman ke paas lekin Poltu usko samjhane mein nakaam hota hai.

Phir kuch din baad usko balcony ke bahar wahi Giddh dikhta hai iss baar woh uske padosi Harilaal ke sarr pe mandrata hai. Poltu phir darwaza kholke Harilaal ke flat jata hai aur uski biwi ko samjhane ki koshish karta hai. Apne dil ke baayi taraf haath rakhke zor zor se Harilaal ki foto dekhke chillata hai lekin uski biwi ko kuch samajh nahi aata woh Jaya ko call karti hai aur Jaya usko Thank You bolti hai.

Agle din Harilaal ka heart fail ho jata hai. Aise karke do teen case ho jaaty hain koi heart attack se koi seedhi se girkay koi car accident se. Aur in sab cases mein Poltu unke marne se ek din pehle unse jaake milta hai aur unko ishara deta hai. Lekin unko samajh nahi aata Jaya ko shaq hota hai key shayad Poltu ko maloom hai kaun iske peechay hai lekin Poltu usko samjhaa nahi paata ke inn sabki wajah kya hai.

Kai din beet jaatay hain who Giddh Poltu ko nahi dikhta aur Poltu wapas se khush ho kerr parindon se khelne lagta hai. Jaya bhi normal ho jaati hai lekin ek shaq zaroor uske dimaag mein atak jaata hai ke Poltu ko shayad inn sabke marne ki wajah maloom hai.

Ek subah Jaya harr din ki tarah office jane ke liye taiiyaar hoti hai. Poltu ka nashta balcony mein rakh ke saaray kaam karke usko bye bolke office ke liye nikalti hai. Poltu apna khushi khushi nashta karta hai aur balcony se Jaya ko bye karta hai theek usi waqt Giddh Jaya ke sarr pe mandrata hua aa jata hai.

Poltu fauran balcony se laga jangla peetnay lagta hai aur gamle mein rakkhay huey patthar bahar ki taraf phenkta hai taaki uski maa ko who rok sakay lekin Jaya uski awaaz sun nahi paati kyuke uske kaan mein ear phone lagay hotay hain aur who music sun rahi hoti hai. Poltu ek paper pe drawing banane lagta hai aur fauran balcony ke bahar ek patther mein bandh karr Jaya ki taraf phenkta hai. lekin Jaya tak woh patthar nahi pahunchta.

Jaya auto leke nikal jaati hai. Poltu rotay rotay baith jata hai. ek banda uss patthar mein bandh paper ko kholke dekhta hai. uss sketch mein ek local train mein blast aur Jaya ki laash aur usme likha hota hai "Amma don't go to office".

AUTHORS' PROFILES

Gautam Sasidharan

Gautam was born in Kerala, spent his toddlerhood in Bihar, studied in Tamil Nadu and is currently working in Hyderabad for the past eleven years. He indulges in managing engineering projects for his daily bread. That said, he satiates his hunger for words by regularly immersing himself in the world set by the different authors he reads and reviewing them on social media platforms. A person who wonders about everything happening around him, he does not restrict himself to any particular genre. His story is an attempt in spinning a fiction around a memory for the readers.

Coordinates: https://gaussreviews.wordpress.com/

www.goodreads.com/user/show/20852494-gautam-sasidharan

gauss86@gmail.com

www.instagram.com/gautamsasidharan/

Krishna Ahir

A stay at home mom by profession, Krishna mesmerizes us with her heart touching, deep poems and stories. She weaves magic through her words and her characters are inspired from real-life incidents. Krishna has been a lifelong writer and first began creating other worlds and characters in her school days. When not absorbed in latest gripping page turner, she loves listening to music and playing with her daughter. She is a Gujju by heart who lives in Hyderabad, with her husband and daughter.

Published Works:
- Psychological Thriller: The Cat Hunter
- https://www.amazon.in/Cat-Hunter-Krishna-Ahir/dp/9389774349/

Short stories and poems in anthologies like
- The Narrow Road Vol 8
- Blooming Tales Vol 1,
- Namaste Ink Magazine Vol 1
- Advent – HydRAW Anthology
- Criticspace Horror Journal Vol 9
- Coffetable Book Vol 1 by Plothera Blogazine

Follow for updates
- Instagram: https://www.instagram.com/author.krishna/

Storymirror:
https://storymirror.com/profile/d7g7gnod/krishna-ahir/stories
https://storymirror.com/profile/d7g7gnod/krishna-ahir/poems

Ravi Theja

Ravi GowriTheja. An author, a poet, an artist, a storyteller, a traveller, a Physics freak and the future farmer. Brat who's gonna be the greatest storyteller.

Pranay Mathur

PranayMathur is a cheerful young author with numerous writing awards to his credit. Passionate about reading, he spends most of his time amidst books. His vivid imagination brings to life a variety of characters, each telling its own unique story. He is a keen Table Tennis player and a keyboard enthusiast.

He can be reached at pranaym2510@gmail.com

Shakeeb Ahmad

Shakeeb, a poet who thinks in Urdu and writes in Roman English. Started his career as radio anchor moved to copy writing and finally working as a creative director in rural market activation. At present he is trying to write, giving shape to moving images in his head and present them like a story.

Muralidharan Parthasarathy

P. Muralidharan, effectively a bilingual, lives in Chennai, India. He has been awarded the Bharathidasan Award for the senior writer. He won the second prize in 2019 for a short story based on the third gender. He stands out in the Modern Tamil literature for more than a decade. His works have been published in renowned literary magazines. He has also translated into Tamil 2 books, including Shashi Tharoor's 'Why I am Hindu'.

Pratima Jaidev

Pratima Jaidev was born in Bhopal, spent initial days of her childhood in Mumbai and the rest of her life in Hyderabad. She is a media professional with 18+ years of work experience across various industry verticals which include the corporate (IT) sector, media houses, educational sector and more; both in India and in the U.S.

Her tenure with reputed firms like Discovery Channel and Voice of America made her realise the lack of soft skills in many new recruits in India. Hence, imbibing soft skills for new joinees based on the needs of their employment has been one of her forte while she held different positions across various industry verticals.

As a filmmaker, she has worked on more than 100+ projects on various subjects, which include documentaries, ads., corporate films and educational videos; for clients of National and International repute. She has also bagged a few awards for her projects.

Currently, she works part time with the Telangana government as a soft skills trainer and is the creative director of her father's three decade old media production company Tarangini Media Works (www.tarangini.co).

She can be reached at **pratima.jaidev@gmail.com**

Ruchi Shrivastava

A software engineer at day and storyteller at night, all thanks to her 4-year-old daughter, Ruchi loves reading all genres. She likes to go on journeys, real and imaginary. Growing up in a small town in Bihar, she thanks her school, which gave her the wings to dream imagination. She is writing fiction stories from her childhood days.

Her inclination to writing is not an overnight one but is the turnout of those writings kept away in folders and drawers. Now, at an adult stage of her life, she wants to take those writings on a serious note to write better and stronger. She now can happily claim to have finally found what makes her heart sing, writing, and more writing.

She believes the power of stories can empower children to grow into wonderful and effective individuals for a diverse world. As a mother, an aspiring children's book author and a software professional, she juggles different roles and responsibilities with equal enthusiasm.

Over the last few years, her essays on Travel and Food have been published in Deccan Herald, Goya Journal. Her essay on gender stereotype was published in eShe online magazine.

She lives in Hyderabad, India since 2012, and love to be part of this city.

Salini Vineeth

Salini Vineeth is a fiction and freelance writer based in Bangalore. After working as an engineer for ten years, Salini quit her job in 2018 to embrace her long time passion for writing. Since then, she has published three books– Magic Square (Novella), Everyday People (Short story collection), and a travel guide for Hampi. Most of her stories depict the dilemmas of modern, urban life. She has a keen interest in history and archaeology. She is also an avid traveller and owns the travel website PickPackGo.in. Salini was born in Wayanad, a quaint hill station in Kerala. She finished her engineering from BITS Goa, and her master's from IIIT-Bangalore. Salini lives in Bangalore with her husband and three-year-old daughter, Tara.

You can find her at https://salinivineeth.in/

https://www.facebook.com/salini.sasidharan.37

salini@ymail.com

Sudheendra Fadnis

Sudheendra Fadnis is a technical writer working for an IT company in Hyderabad. He identifies himself as a person with an insatiable curiosity. A voracious reader by nature with an omnivorous taste for wide ranging subjects such as psychology, history, poetry and philosophy. He reads almost anything that piques his curiosity; mostly non-fiction. He started his reading journey with Victorian classics during his teenage years, and then went on to explore other subjects of his interest. He is greatly inspired by the works of Nassim Taleb and Fredreich Nietzsche. He looks up to Sir Winston Churchill and above all, his late father

Dedication: *I dedicate this story in the loving memory of my father, who was not just a father to me but a hero, friend, philosopher, guide, mentor, icon and much more. He was the one who always believed in my abilities no matter what. I owe all my merits and talents to him. Love you Appa! Miss you forever.*

Credits: *This story would not have come from me without the encouragement from Krishna Ahir. It is she who ignited the idea in me that I should leverage on my knowledge that I have gained by reading neuroscience books to pen down a story like this. Thank you very much Krishna, will be grateful always for being so encouraging.*

Swapnil Saurav

Swapnil earns his living by working in Software Industry and solving customers' problems. He has spent over 16 years in various industries like Healthcare, Retail and Manufacturing. He started writing in the year 2013 with Technology books and in 2018, he also started writing Fiction stories and novels. He writes about common people and describes things which can happen in anybody's life. His list of publications can be found at: www.amazon.com/author/swapnil

He can be contacted at: callswapnil@gmail.com

CURATORS' PROFILES

Sirisha Naidu

Sirisha works with a media firm, where she engages closely with the marginalized communities like farmers, weavers, tribals and brings out their stories in the form of short films. She loves to travel across remote villages in the country, interact with the locals and eat local cuisine.

Aruna Kumar

Arun, by choice, joined the library profession, with qualifications for teaching. He has been in the library profession for more than 22 years and has been working with children for more than 18 years. Reading is his passion. Attending various literary events and sharing his experiences in social media made him believe in lifelong learning and a positive attitude towards life. Arun was in the curation team for the HydRAW's anthology Coronicles. He is also on the publication team / editorial team of School Librarians Association, India.

His social media coordinates are:

Goodreads - Aruna Kumar Gadepalli

Blog -- http://arunaschoolib.blogspot.com

LinkedIn -- https://www.linkedin.com/in/aruna-kumar-gadepalli-68409910

EDITOR'S PROFILE

Lavanya Nukavarapu

Lavanya Nukavarapu is a finance professional who used to deliberate only on finance until one day poems and stories beckoned her. She became a compulsive writer who could not go to sleep without penning at least a few words every day. Her first book Bare Thoughts, a collection of her poems was published in 2018. In 2019, Lavanya published her first novel, The Captive, a psychological thriller that has received outstanding reviews. Her second novel Cigarettes Sex Love published in 2020 explores the complexities of modern-day relationships.

A research paper on Bare Thoughts, The 21st Century Perspectives in the Poems by Lavanya Nukavarapu was presented in February, 2020 by Prof. Sumalya Mali of Saldiha College, Bankura (W.B.) at the seminar "Recent Trends in Indian Women's Literature" organised by Midnapore College, Midnapore, West Bengal.

She is also a professional editor and likes to help upcoming authors in editing/guiding their works and promoting new talent. Her prior editing works include a historical fiction novel, a self-help and a political thriller.

You can follow her on social media:

https://www.facebook.com/lavanya.nukavarapu

https://www.instagram.com/lavanya_nukavarapu

https://www.amazon.in/Lavanya-Nukavarapu/e/B07KX45WJH

You can email her at lavanya.nukas@gmail.com in case you want to reach her for professional assignments.